S0-AQC-550

Pete gently turned Bess around. She faced him and smiled. He bent toward her, and she tilted her face up to meet his kiss. She tried not to think about anything as she felt his lips graze her neck and gently tug at her earlobe. He was a wonderful kisser—so much more inventive and self-assured than Lenny. Still, she was angry with herself for thinking about Lenny, even while Pete was kissing her. . . .

STRICTLY PERSONAL

Phyllis Schieber

FAWCETT JUNIPER • NEW YORK

*In memory of my father, who would
have been the least surprised
and the most proud—
you still make me laugh.*

Acknowledgments

The author gives very special thanks to Hayes B. Jacobs for
always insisting she push herself just a little bit harder and for
always making believe she could; and to Liane Kupferberg
Carter for doing last minute revisions, making valuable
suggestions, and cheering her on.

RLI: $\dfrac{\text{VL: } 5 + \text{up}}{\text{IL: } 10 + \text{up}}$

A Fawcett Juniper Book
Published by Ballantine Books
Copyright © 1987 by Phyllis Schieber

All rights reserved under International and Pan-American Copyright
Conventions. Published in the United States by Ballantine Books, a
division of Random House, Inc., New York, and simultaneously in Canada
by Random House of Canada Limited, Toronto.

Library of Congress Catalog Card Number: 87-91018

ISBN 0-449-70230-8

All the characters in this book are fictitious, and any resemblance to
persons living or dead is purely coincidental.

Manufactured in the United States of America

First Edition: January 1988

Chapter 1

"There must be something wrong with me," Bess said, prying the rock loose from the dirt with the tip of her sneakered foot.

Margaret was trying to resume a normal breathing pattern. She had unwillingly agreed to begin jogging with Bess.

Still unable to speak, Margaret shook her head. She had never known two miles could be quite that long.

"Then what is it?" Bess said.

Margaret shrugged.

"You can't be *that* tired."

Margaret nodded, rolling her eyes in confirmation.

"C'mon. You'll feel better."

"That, I doubt."

They got up from the bench and slowly headed down the jogging trail. Puffing joggers of all ages passed by with playful remarks. "Give up already?" one man said. "Can't take it?" an elderly woman teased.

"Up yours," Margaret said. She limped alongside Bess's long, easy strides.

Bess giggled and draped her arm across her friend's shoulder.

1

"You're getting better, Meg."

"Better than what?"

"Better than the last time you went jogging."

Margaret looked skeptical.

"This is the first time I've been jogging," she said.

"You see!" Bess said. "You're better already."

Margaret playfully shoved Bess.

"So far," Margaret said, "the only thing I've lost is twenty-four dollars for a lousy pair of running shoes.

"And I don't think I've ever seen a nicer pair in my life."

Margaret stuck her tongue out at Bess. It was an old habit. They had been friends since kindergarten and fell easily into a familiar routine of teasing.

"Why am I killing myself?" Margaret said. "What's the point? Why can't I live my life without tendonitis? Don't I have enough burdens to shoulder?"

Bess laughed as Margaret waved her arms and raised her head to the sky. Margaret wanted to be an actress—she wanted the lead in the school play and was trying to lose ten pounds. Bess thought it was a good idea to lose the weight anyway, but she didn't tell that to Margaret.

"Well?" Margaret said. "Hasn't life already given me enough trials and tribulations? Must I now add shin splints to the list of injustices?"

Bess turned to look at Margaret's flushed face. Her blonde hair, a shade darker from dampness, clung to her forehead, setting off her beautiful skin. A fine line of perspiration glistened on her upper lip. In spite of being slightly chubby, Margaret was a striking girl. The long looks she got from passing men always made Bess uneasy, but Margaret didn't seem to notice. For that matter, neither did the boys in their class—they only noticed the extra pounds.

"Quit clowning," Bess said. "You're the one who wants to lose weight."

"Moi?" Margaret said with exaggerated surprise. *"Moi?* I would rather be home this fine Sunday morning, dipping chunks of French toast in pools of maple syrup and butter. That's what *moi* would like to be doing!"

2

Bess made a face and shook her head.

"You'll feel better after you lose ten pounds."

"I feel better already, Coach," Margaret said. "I just wonder what's in all this for you. After all, *you're* the American heartthrob—long and lean."

"What do you mean?" Bess said.

"Well, being thin doesn't seem to have made you any happier."

Bess bristled. She knew that Margaret was referring to Lenny. Lately things hadn't been going very smoothly between Bess and Lenny. He was a nice boy. Bess's mother used those exact words to describe him. Bess's father called Lenny "a good kid." He really was. He was a good student and an excellent athlete. Lenny was a year ahead of Bess in school and would be going off to college next year. Several college scouts had already been out to observe Lenny's wrestling abilities. He was sure to get a scholarship. He was also eighteen and more than curious about all the locker room stories he heard from the other boys. "Not that I'm pushing you," he had told Bess after their last date. "I'd just like to have a smug look on my face instead of that hopeful expression I always seem to have." Bess had laughed at Lenny's hangdog look, but she had begged off early that night, claiming to be coming down with something. Lenny hadn't believed her.

Margaret waited for Bess's response, but she was intently observing the weekend crowd that routinely invaded Cental Park.

"Bess?"

Bess knew that Margaret was waiting for an answer. It seemed as if *everyone* was waiting for something, especially Lenny.

"It has nothing to do with happiness," Bess said. "If you lose weight, it'll be one less thing to worry about."

Bess had a habit of picking up conversations as if time hadn't passed. Margaret had learned how to follow her friend's thoughts without losing the rhythm of the conversation.

"What are you worrying about?" Margaret said.

Bess stopped for a minute to consider Margaret's question. Bess tilted her face to meet the sun's warmth. Although it was cold for October, it was easy to remember the summer if you stood directly in the sun's path. With her eyes closed against the glare, Bess saw colors sparkle in front of her tightly shut eyelids. It reminded her of the kaleidoscope she used to have—she had spent hours turning and twisting the dial. Bess loved the way the sun felt against her skin. She wrenched herself away from both the warmth of the sun and the warmth of her memories—things were much safer inside her head. She deliberately avoided Margaret's question. They continued walking.

"Are we going to keep walking until you answer me?" Margaret said. "If we are, I'd rather take a cab."

Bess was annoyed with Margaret's prodding. Didn't she know that Bess just didn't feel like talking about it? Why couldn't everyone just leave her alone for a while? Bess decided to throw the conversation off on to another track— she had spoken to her brother the night before. Sam was a sophomore at Boston University. Margaret had been in love with him since they had met. It was something Bess often kidded Margaret about, although they both knew it wasn't a joke.

"I spoke to Sam yesterday," Bess said.

"Low blow," Margaret said. She shook her head. "I'm surprised at you, Bessie. You could have said you didn't feel like talking."

Bess was all innocence.

"What are you talking about?" she said.

Margaret blushed but bent to pick up a twig and began peeling the bark. She tried to appear nonchalant.

"So, how's he doin'?"

Bess was immediately contrite. It *had* been a rotten diversion to use on Margaret. She couldn't hide her interest even though she was angry at Bess for using Sam to change the subject.

"He's fine," Bess said. "He loves school. Can you imagine anyone loving school?"

Margaret laughed, but she kept her head bent over the twig.

"Does he love anything or anyone else?" Margaret said.

Bess decided not to mention Sam's new love. "She's from Texas," he had said. "She looks like a Dallas cheerleader."

"No," Bess said. "You know Sam. He never gets into that stuff. He'll be home for Thanksgiving—I'll pump him then."

"Speaking of pumping," Margaret said. "Can we return to the original subject?"

"Not now," Bess said. "Let's jog some more."

They jogged in silence. They were both busy with their own thoughts. As close as they were, they were still separate. While their lives were filled with endless variables, their friendship was a constant. It made it possible for them to push into each other's secret corners without fear of creating a disturbance.

Reaching the entrance to the park, they slowed their pace to a comfortable walk. They collapsed on a bench, huffing and puffing with exaggerated exhaustion. The sun had disappeared behind the clouds, and there was a sharp chill in the air.

"Now?" Margaret said.

Bess turned to look at Margaret—they smiled at each other.

"Persistent, aren't we?" Bess said. "I don't know, Meg. Everything seems so mixed up. I can't explain it."

Margaret pushed her hair out of her eyes and reached over to touch Bess's hand lightly.

"Try," Margaret said. "You'll feel better."

Bess looked unsure and sighed.

"Lenny's been pushing," she said. "He says he's not, but he is."

"And?"

5

"And, I just don't know."

"Do you love him?" Margaret said.

Bess looked into Margaret's eyes.

"Do I have to?" Bess said.

The question made them both quiet for a moment. Margaret broke the silence.

"I understand it makes a big difference," she said.

Bess laughed.

"I meant," she said, "if I love him, do I have to sleep with him?"

This time they both laughed.

"Damn it," Margaret said. "I certainly don't know."

Bess knew Margaret must be thinking about Sam.

"Well, who does know?" Bess said.

"You're the only person who can decide," Margaret said. "You have to figure it out."

"I was never good at puzzles," Bess said. "Never. Do you remember those puzzle pages in the funnies section of the Sunday paper?"

"Why do you always change the subject?" Margaret said.

"I'm not changing the subject. I'm trying to be deep. Well, do you remember?"

Margaret nodded. She narrowed her blue eyes to two small slits—a sign that she was listening but not yet following Bess's train of thought.

"I used to save that page for the end. I didn't have much trouble with the word jumbles," Bess said. "I zipped through those."

"Bess, could you get to the point?"

"Patience, my dear. There was this one puzzle—I think it was called 'What's Wrong with This Picture?'—do you remember what it was called?"

Margaret slumped over with her hands on her chest.

"You're killing me, Bess."

"All right. Well, I always had trouble with that one. I was sure I would never be able to find the mistakes.

Everything always looked fine to me. Finally I would notice that the man in the picture was missing an ear, that the chair had five legs, that the cat didn't have any whiskers, and that *sugar* was spelled with an *e* instead of an *a*. It always took me a while to figure it out."

"Is there a point to this trip down memory lane?" Margaret said. "Is our first-grade teacher going to step out from behind those bushes?"

"Could you be serious for a minute?" Bess said. "I'm trying to make a point."

"Try harder."

"The point is," Bess said, "I didn't understand that if you want to see what's wrong with something, you have to look at all the individual parts of the picture."

Margaret's face was blank. She had never gotten used to Bess's weird way of explaining the simplest things.

"And?" Margaret said.

"And," Bess said, "I still can't see the separate pictures. You know what I mean?"

Margaret grinned.

"What's so funny?" Bess said.

"Does this mean that you don't want to sleep with Lenny? Or does it mean you want to work on puzzles with him?"

"It means you're a jerk," Bess said.

"Can you explain that, please?" Margaret said. She stopped for a minute and quickly added, "Forget I said that. One explanation from you a day is more than I can handle."

Bess lunged at Margaret, but Margaret had already anticipated Bess's move. They ran down the street laughing, with Bess shouting promises of "Wait till I get you!" Up to that moment she had managed to forget about Lenny, but her own words suddenly reminded her that he was due to arrive at seven o'clock that evening.

Chapter 2

Margaret knew that Bess wasn't telling her everything about what was going on with Lenny. These last few weeks, Bess had been moody and distracted. Still, Margaret couldn't help feeling resentful. After all, Lenny was one of the most popular boys in the school. Bess always seemed to get the right guys without even making an effort. It had been that way as long as they had known each other.

Although the streets were jammed with joggers, Margaret couldn't help feeling self-conscious in her sweat suit and sneakers. She looked as if she should be jogging, while everyone else looked sleek and ahtletic. She trudged up Broadway with her hands stuck deep down in her pockets and caught a glimpse of herself in a store window.

"Alas, poor Margaret," she said aloud.

No one even turned around—it was not unusual for people to talk to themselves on the streets of New York. Margaret savored her momentary anonymity and softly rehearsed her lines for her part as Ophelia in the school play. She was almost positive that she would get the role. Mr. Rand, the drama coach, had as much as said so. "Margaret," Mr. Rand had said, "you would make a perfectly exquisite Ophelia. Of course, ten pounds less of you would guarantee Ophelia's honor."

"What a diplomat," Margaret now mumbled. "I'll give him honor. 'Could beauty, my lord, have better commerce than with honesty?'"

Margaret noticed that the only person to regard her outburst dubiously was a poor old bag lady. Margaret gave her a thumbs-up sign and a broad grin.

Saturday shoppers were everywhere, hauling bags of exotic delicacies from the local stores. Broadway was an international food festival—Italian sausages, Chinese pressed duck, Jamaican meat pies, Latin *cuchifritos,* and dark Jewish ryes seemed to beckon Margaret. She studied the faces of the people in the hurrying crowds and wondered whom their purchases were for—boyfriends, husbands, lovers? Margaret thought of Bess getting ready for her date with Lenny, and a sudden stab of animosity stopped her dead in her tracks.

"'Oh, help me, you sweet Heavens!'" Margaret said, raising her hands to the darkening sky. She clasped her clenched fists to her chest and threw back her head.

Bess had tried to convince Margaret to join her and Lenny that night. "We're just going to the movies," Bess had said. "Why don't you come?" The suggestion had been well intended, but Margaret had insisted that she had to study her lines for Monday's audition. Her face had burned with shame at the look in Bess's dark eyes—there wasn't even a hint of malice in them. Margaret had carefully searched her friend's face.

It wasn't as if Margaret hadn't been to the movies with Bess and Lenny before. Margaret had rarely watched the picture, concentrating all her efforts on ignoring Lenny's hand massaging Bess's shoulder or the way their fingers seemed to be laced together. Their dark heads often bent together to whisper something to each other, and their soft laughter always filled her with envy. Bess and Lenny were always concerned and attentive about Margaret. They wanted her to have a good time, but she never did. Margaret just wasn't in the mood to face another evening of their good cheer.

She was glad when she finally reached her building. Before she even turned the key in the door, she could smell her mother's stew simmering on the stove.

"Margaret?" her mother said. "Where have you been? Bess called ages ago. I was worried."

"Bess? What did she want?"

"Where have you been?"

"What did she want?"

"We seem to be having two different conversations," her mother said. Alice Manning was an older, chubbier version of her daughter. Her dark blond hair fell in wisps onto her pink cheeks. Her blue eyes were like two metallic disks framed by almost invisible lashes. Her softly rounded chin was a testimony to her refusal to follow fashion. "I like to eat," she always said. "What can I do?"

"What did Bess want?" Margaret repeated. She followed her mother into the kitchen and started lifting lids off the pots. "Smells good."

"It is good."

"I was walking."

"I thought you were jogging."

"I was walking after I was jogging."

"You must have worked up an appetite."

"Exercise decreases your appetite." Margaret's voice didn't hold much conviction.

"Nonsense," her mother said.

"Did Bess want me to call her back?"

Her mother had reentered the rhythm of her cooking. She was peeling potatoes with deft, swift movements. She turned to look at Margaret, but her fingers kept up their steady motion.

"Watch your fingers," Margaret said. She let the tap water run and tested its temperature with one finger.

10

"I guess I could peel potatoes with my eyes closed. And yes, Bess said to call her back."

Margaret drank a glass of water in great, greedy gulps while her mother dropped the peeled potatoes in a pot of water.

"Your father is closing the shop early tonight. We have opera tickets. God only knows why I agreed to an opera, but you know your father. Janie is sleeping over at Karen's tonight—I dropped her off this afternoon. You'll have the house all to yourself."

"I won't be alone."

"Oh?"

"The Prince of Denmark is coming."

"Again?" her mother said. "He was just here."

"He likes me. He finds me alluring." Margaret put one hand behind her head and one hand on her hip, thrusting her pelvis forward.

Her mother looked at her over a cup of coffee. She always had a cup close at hand and took sips from it throughout the day. She never seemed to mind that the coffee was cold—in fact, she preferred it that way.

"I wish you'd spend your time with someone your own age," she said. She set the cup on the counter with a thud as if to emphasize her point.

"Mother, please don't start."

"I'm not starting, dear. I'm merely expressing an opinion."

"You're starting."

"I give up."

"I consider that a victory," Margaret said. "I'm going to call Bess."

Margaret kicked off her sneakers and stretched out across her bed. There were dozens of stuffed animals and dolls lined up against the wall. She refused to part with any of them. Her younger sister, Jane, had inherited a few of Margaret's less favorite ones, but the parting had been

11

painful and forced. Margaret looked affectionately at her one-eyed teddy bear.

Bess answered on the first ring—her voice was breathless.

"Hello?" Bess said.

"Hi."

"Where were you? I was worried. You said you were going straight home."

"Stop making noises like a mother," Margaret said. She pulled her teddy bear close and played with his floppy ears.

"What's that supposed to mean?" Bess said.

"Aren't you late?"

"Lenny's not here yet. Anyway, I'm not even dressed."

"Good for you. Bad for Lenny."

"Now, what's *that* supposed to mean?"

"We don't seem to be communicating," Margaret said. There was silence on the other end of the line.

"Hello?" Margaret said. "Hel-lo, are you there?"

"I'm here . . . I wish you were here, too."

"Why?"

Margaret wound the telephone cord around the teddy bear's neck in a noose—she held the ends of the cord together at the back of his head and pulled upward. The bear's head flopped pathetically to one side, and Margaret felt strangely satisfied. She let her own tongue dangle out of her mouth. Bess had been talking all through this, but Margaret had allowed her thoughts to wander.

". . . and we'll probably stop for a hamburger later. You should really come. We'll meet up with some other kids from school. Zak will probably be there. Won't you change your mind?" Bess said.

"I'm sorry. I wasn't really listening."

"For God's sake, Margaret. What's with you?"

"What did you say about Zak?"

"I said we would probably run into him later on."

"So?"

12

"You know he likes you. He can't take his eyes off you in English class."

"It's not me he's looking at. He just focuses on something and goes into a comatose state."

"I give up. You're impossible."

"Aha! My second victory, and the night's still young."

"What are you talking about?"

Margaret could hear Bess's front doorbell ring—it was a muffled yet intrusive sound.

"You'd better go," Margaret said. "I'll speak to you tomorrow. Have a good time."

She slammed down the phone before Bess had a chance to say anything more. Margaret closed her eyes for a few seconds and tried to picture Zak. He was a shy, studious boy with a sharp nose and curly red hair. When the image had taken shape, she bolted upright and flung the bear across the room. He landed with a thud against her dresser.

"'He is dead and gone/At his head a grass-green turf/At his heels a stone,'" Margaret said in a singsong voice. "'Oh, oh!'"

She sat on the edge of her bed and held her head in her hands. She thought about Bess and Lenny and all the other kids from school—they would all be trying to outdo one another with jokes and stories. Margaret sighed and stood. Without even bothering to shower and change, she pulled a piece of stationery from her desk drawer and sat down.

"Dear Sam," she began, saying the words aloud as she wrote. "Bess told me you would be coming home for Thanksgiving. I was really happy to hear that. It's been so long since I have seen you. Bess says you are really enjoying school. She didn't mention anything about your love life even though I asked."

Margaret stopped and reread what she had written. Mockingly, she shouted, "Bess said! Bess said!" She crumpled up the paper and thought longingly of Sam.

"I'm just Bess's best friend," Margaret said. "'Lord, we know what we are but know not why we may be.'"

13

Margaret picked up a copy of her script and thumbed quickly through the pages. She wondered if she was taking the role of Ophelia too seriously. She picked up her teddy bear from the floor and hugged him close to her chest.

"I'll drown my sorrows," Margaret said. "But I definitely won't drown myself."

Chapter 3

The first thing Bess noticed about Lenny was the way he avoided her eyes. He was polite enough to her parents, Carl and Ruth. He even laughed at her father's corny jokes. Still, Bess could see it was an effort for him. He even refused a piece of her mother's apple pie. "Are you feeling well?" Ruth couldn't help but ask. Lenny only nodded and smiled. Finally, Bess felt it was time to leave.

"I'm ready," she said.

"Great," Lenny said. "Let's go."

"Nice to see you again," Carl said, rising from his chair to shake Lenny's hand.

"Thank you," Lenny said. He shifted uncomfortably from one foot to the other.

"Good night, Daddy," Bess said. "I won't be late."

Bess and Lenny collided as they walked out the front door. Each stepped aside to let the other pass and walked into each other for a second time. Earlier in their relationship they would have collapsed with laughter, hugging each other and reminding themselves to remember the moment. Instead they looked at each other awkwardly and tried to hide their discomfort.

"We seem to be getting in each other's way," Bess said.

Lenny seemed not to have heard her.

They walked to the bus stop in silence, their hands in their pockets, huddled inside themselves against the chill air. Bess pulled up her collar and shivered.

"It got cold quickly," she said. "It was much warmer this morning."

"Uh-huh."

"Uh-huh? That's all you have to say?" Bess was trying to tease him out of his mood.

"Sorry, Bessie. I was thinking."

She tucked her arm through his and playfully rested her head against his wool sleeve.

"I'll bet I know about what."

Lenny's arm felt stiff, and he didn't answer. Bess withdrew her hand.

"What time does the movie start?" she said.

They were both Woody Allen buffs and were headed down to the Village for a double feature of his earlier works.

"We have plenty of time," Lenny said. He looked embarrassed and quickly added, "For the movie, I mean. Well, it's eight-fifteen. I think. I'm not sure."

Bess looked at him and suddenly felt afraid. They reached the bus stop and took their place with a handful of waiting people, peering anxiously up the avenue. It always made Bess laugh to see people craning their necks in the same direction. It was just like people staring at the numbers in an elevator.

"Wouldn't it be funny to look in the opposite direction?" she said.

"You *always* say the same thing."

Bess knew she did, but it had always made Lenny laugh.

"Sorry," she said.

"No, I'm sorry."

"What's the matter, Len?" Her voice was soft and concerned.

Lenny looked down at her and smiled. He touched her cheek with the back of his hand.

"You look very pretty," he said. "You always look very pretty."

Bess reached up and grabbed his head. She pressed it to her face.

"I love you," she said. "I really do."

"The bus is here." He moved his hand and guided her into the bus.

Neither of them laughed much during *Sleeper* or *Bananas*, their two favorite movies. Bess was conscious of the way Lenny didn't touch her—he didn't even put his arm around her. Once their hands brushed as they simultaneously reached for popcorn. Lenny stared at the screen although Bess was sure he must have felt her looking at him. She slumped down in her seat and tried not to cry. It was clear that Lenny had something on his mind, and she was sure it wasn't anything she wanted to hear.

It was after midnight when the movie let out. The streets of Greenwich Village were just beginning to come alive. Bess checked her watch—she was allowed to be home at one-thirty on a Saturday.

"Where are we supposed to meet everyone?" she said.

"Oh, the souvlaki place, I think. I wasn't really in the mood."

"Oh?"

"I thought we'd go someplace where we could be alone. Get a pizza or something."

Bess would have preferred the noisy gaiety of their friends. Still, she knew it was inevitable that Lenny would say whatever was on his mind. Stalling wouldn't do either of them any good.

"Fine," she said. "Pizza sounds good."

"Are you hungry?" Lenny said.

"Starved."

"You're always starved."

Bess felt a pang, realizing how well they knew each other. She had grown lazy with the ease of their relationship. She allowed Lenny to steer her across the busy street.

17

The lights in the pizza shop glared with neon obtrusiveness. They both blinked and stood silently in the doorway. Lenny indicated a corner table with a thrust of his chin. Bess took a seat while Lenny approached the counter to place their order.

He doesn't even have to ask me what I want, Bess thought.

Lenny brought two Cokes to the table and returned to the counter to wait for their slices. Bess watched him as he leaned against the ledge, talking easily to the owner. She couldn't hear what they were saying, but she liked the way Lenny's face was so intent—he was a good listener. His long fingers picked idly at something, but his eyes never left the man's face. The owner slid the pizza from the oven and expertly sliced it. Lenny walked toward the table, balancing the slices and a shaker of hot pepper.

"All set," he said. "One well-done slice." He took a seat across from Bess.

"I feel like this is my last meal," Bess said. "Do I get a blindfold?"

Lenny looked as if he were going to cry.

"Don't make this harder for me," he said.

All the tenderness Bess had previously felt for him disappeared and was replaced by anger.

"I was just joking," she said. "Obviously, you're not."

Lenny's mouth was open, getting ready to take his first big bite. His mouth remained open and empty—wordless.

"Well," she said. "Get it over with. How bad could it be? Is it college? Have you decided to go out of town? Whatever it is, let's stop playing this silly game."

She knew she was babbling. It couldn't be college. She wished it were something as simple, but she knew it wasn't.

"It has nothing to do with college," Lenny said.

"Are we going to have another talk about sex?"

"Damn it. Why can't you be serious? No. I'm tired of *talking* about sex to you. If you must know . . . I want to have it instead."

18

"So that's what this is all about."

Lenny put his pizza down and wiped his mouth.

"Well?" Bess said. "Let's hear it. You're not pregnant, are you?"

She hated herself for being so childish, but she wanted to shield herself from what she knew was coming. She had an urge to raise her arms and cover her face to protect herself. It was a pity you couldn't protect yourself from words.

"Stop it," Lenny said. "Let's talk."

Bess looked directly at him. He fiddled with his napkin, rolling it tightly and quickly releasing it. She felt as if she were watching a movie of herself in slow motion.

"You know how much our friendship means to me," Lenny said.

The word *friendship* meant she was in serious trouble. She wished she could reach up and snatch the word from the air. Lock it away somewhere and pretend it had never been uttered. How strange it would be not to see Lenny anymore—Lenny, her "friend."

"It's just that I think it would be best if we saw other people for a while," Lenny said. "Healthier for both of us."

"How thoughtful of you to think of me. What if I don't think it's *healthier* for me?"

"It's important for me."

"Is it just the sex?" Bess said. "Is it really just the sex?"

"No," Lenny said. "It's more than that. I need to get some balance. I feel as if I'm not in control anymore—of myself, I mean."

Bess understood. She didn't like it, but she understood. Still, she felt awful.

"Do you understand?" Lenny said.

"About balance? I guess so. I keep thinking about when I first learned to ride a bike."

"Why? What does that have to do with us?"

"Nothing . . . and everything. It has to do with me."

Lenny searched Bess's face, and she continued talking.

19

"My father spent weeks trying to teach me how to ride. He used training wheels and everything. Finally, he tried running after me, holding the seat of the bike. I thought I could do it, but I kept looking back to make sure he was still there. One time, I looked back and he was at the other end of the block. He was waving at me and jumping up and down. As soon as I realized he'd let go, I fell. I was furious. 'I thought you were ready,' he told me. Well, I wasn't. I guess I'm not ready for this, either. So please, Len. Don't talk to me about balance."

"You're not being fair," he said.

"*I'm* not being fair? How can you say that? You spring this on me from nowhere. You talk to me about balance and control and give me the friendship bit. Really, at least be honest with me. You want sex, and I won't do it with you. Have you already found someone for the seduction?"

Lenny blushed and drew his hands into two fists.

Bess slapped her head with her hand. "How stupid of me! I don't believe it! You really have found someone."

"It's not like that. I just need some space."

"Space? God, how corny."

"Bess, we'll always be friends."

"*Always?* That's an awfully long time."

Lenny reached across the table to take her hands. She recoiled from his touch.

"I'd like to go home," she said.

They rose in unison as if in mockery of their very separateness. Walking toward the door, Bess stumbled and instinctively reached for the hand Lenny offered her.

"I'm all right," she said. "I guess I'm still checking to see if someone is back there."

Lenny started to say something, but Bess cut him off.

"Don't. Please. You know me. I need time to think things over. I still haven't forgiven my father for letting go."

Lenny's startled look gave her an enormous feeling of satisfaction.

Chapter 4

Bess didn't want to open her eyes. She pulled the covers up over her head to block out the light that was streaming in through the venetian blinds she had forgotten to close the night before. Last night—the memory of the evening was brought back to her. She didn't feel like facing anything right now. She could hear her parents' voices in the kitchen. The smell of fresh coffee was inviting. She kicked off the blankets and sat up in bed. Lenny smiled at her from an eight-by-ten glossy on the dresser. She shivered even though it wasn't cold.

"What the hell are you smiling at?" Bess said. She hurled her pillow across the room, hitting Lenny squarely in the face. The picture crashed to the floor, but it didn't break. The noise brought her mother hurrying to the door.

"Bess? Are you all right?" Her mother opened the door and thrust her concerned face inside. "Did you fall?"

Bess was feeling around under the bed for her slippers. She hated them, but she knew her mother would go off into a long speech about arthritis if Bess didn't wear them. She took her robe off a hook on the back of the door and smiled at her mother.

"I'm okay, Mom. Really."

"What happened?"

"Nothing. Just a wild burst of passion. You know how emotional teenagers are."

Her mother laughed, and Bess felt relieved. She didn't feel like getting into a heavy discussion about last night.

"Come have some breakfast," her mother said. "I was just making some pancakes."

"I'll be right there."

Bess looked at her reflection in the bathroom mirror. She was startled to see that she looked the same as she had yesterday. She pulled down the corners of her mouth and made her eyelids droop.

"There!" she said. "Now you look properly pathetic."

She washed her face and brushed her teeth, concentrating on being cheerful with her parents.

Her father was thumbing through the Sunday paper and drinking coffee. Her mother was carefully watching the pancakes as they bubbled on the griddle.

"Good morning," Bess said.

Her father looked up from the paper and smiled.

"Rough night?" Carl said.

Bess poured herself a cup of coffee without looking at either of her parents. It was too soon to tell them that she and Lenny were through. She needed time. Suddenly she felt like talking to Sam.

"Is it all right if I call Sam?" she said. "The rates are cheaper on Sunday."

"Of course," her mother said. "Don't you want to eat first?"

"I'm not hungry."

"Keep it short," her father said.

Bess took her cup of coffee into her room. Sam answered the phone on the third ring.

"Sam? It's me."

"Bess? What are you doing up so early?"

"I couldn't sleep."

"What's up? You sound somewhat less than your usual cheery self."

22

"I am somewhat less than my usual cheery self."

"What happened?"

Bess suddenly felt embarrassed. She struggled for a way to ease herself into the conversation.

"Nothing—that's the problem, I think."

"You're not making any sense."

"Lenny broke up with me."

"Wh-at? I don't believe it. Not the Romeo and Juliet of Manhattan's West Side."

Bess had forgotten how insensitive Sam could sometimes be.

"I said he broke up with me. I didn't say we made a suicide pact."

"Sorry."

"Could you just listen and not be so stupid? I need to talk about it."

"I said I was sorry. What happened? He must have given you a reason."

"Oh, he did. He gave me one very big reason—sex."

"Sex?"

"Sex," Bess said. "Or, actually, the absence of it."

"Oh."

"'Oh'?" Bess said. "I call you long distance for some advice, and all you can say is 'oh'?"

"What do you want me to say? The two of you have been seeing each other a long time. I guess I thought you were sleeping together."

"*Really?*"

"Why do you sound so surprised? That's the way things are. I'm not telling you anything you don't already know."

"Are you telling me to sleep with Lenny?"

"I'm not telling you to do anything," Sam said. "I'm just telling you that I'm not surprised it's an issue."

She was too surprised to think of an answer.

"Are you still there?" Sam said.

"I'm here."

Her voice sounded disembodied.

"Let me explain," Sam said.

"I wish you would."

"In many ways things are very tough for guys today. A lot of girls don't have any problem about sleeping with a guy."

"It sounds really tough to be a guy."

"Give me a chance. The problem is that it's difficult to stick with a girl who won't sleep with you when there are girls who will—even if you like the girl a lot."

"Lenny told me he loved me."

"Maybe that makes it harder."

"I don't understand that," Bess said. "It just doesn't make sense."

"I'm sorry. I haven't been much help."

"I just can't be something I'm not," Bess said. "I just can't."

"Then that's your answer."

"I guess so, but I don't feel good about it. Anyway, I'll speak to you soon."

"I just want to tell you one more thing."

"What?"

Bess tried to keep the edge of impatience out of her voice. She was eager to get off the phone. It had been a mistake to call Sam—she should have called Margaret.

"Maybe," Sam said, "Lenny just wasn't the right one."

"No. I don't think it has anything to do with Lenny. I'll speak to you soon."

Bess hung up before Sam had a chance to say anything. She sat for a few minutes before calling Margaret, trying to sort out everything Sam had said. She would have to be careful about how she expressed Sam's views to Margaret— it was a touchy situation. The phone rang, interrupting her thoughts. Bess picked it up on the first ring, certain that it was Margaret.

"I was just about to call you," Bess said.

"I'm glad."

Bess was startled to hear Lenny's voice.

"Oh," Bess said. "It's you."

"You don't sound thrilled."

"What do you want?"

"I wanted to make sure you were all right. I was worried about you."

Bess didn't answer.

"I should have prepared you," Lenny said. "I didn't know how. I didn't want to hurt you."

Bess still didn't answer.

"I care a lot about you," Lenny said.

"Look," Bess said, "we went through all this last night. I'm sure it's all for the best."

"I'm glad you feel that way, because there's something else I had to tell you."

Bess braced herself for the bomb.

"I wanted to tell you before someone else did," Lenny said.

Bess waited.

"I'm sort of dating Ellen Duncan."

Bess drew in a sharp breath. She couldn't believe it. Ellen Duncan just wasn't Lenny's type—at least, not the Lenny she thought she knew.

"Is that all you wanted to tell me?" Bess said.

"I just didn't want you to find out from someone else."

"That was very thoughtful of you. Good-bye."

Bess hung up and flung herself across her bed. It was just too much to believe. First, that awful conversation with Sam. Now, this baring of Lenny's soul. The absolute worst part was finding out that she had been dumped for Ellen Duncan.

"It's just too humiliating," Bess said aloud. "I lost out to a cheerleader with big pom-poms."

As funny as it all seemed, Bess just couldn't stop crying.

Chapter 5

Bess was having trouble spearing the lo mein with her chopsticks. Disgustedly she pushed the carton away and watched Margaret.

"How can you still be hungry?" Bess said.

Margaret continued eating without taking her eyes from Bess's face.

"I'm hungry," Margaret said. "I haven't eaten all day."

An assortment of containers covered the coffee table in Margaret's living room. Packets of oily, black soy sauce and gooey duck sauce were scattered among the remains of their dinner. Margaret scraped the bottom of her container and sighed contentedly.

"I love Chinese food," she said. "I must have been Chinese in a former life." She peered into another container. "Are you going to finish this?" she said.

Bess shook her head.

"How can you eat?" she said. "My whole life is falling apart, and you're stuffing your face."

"I always eat in a time of crisis," Margaret said. "Anyway, discussions about sex make me ravenous."

Bess uncurled her legs from beneath her and arched her back.

"My damned leg fell asleep. I feel so miserable."

"Shake it around. You'll feel better."

Bess rolled her eyes.

"It's not my leg, stupid. It's my life."

"I know. I thought a little humor would get your mind off things."

Margaret stood and started collecting the containers, making sure that they were all empty.

"Do you want some tea?"

Bess nodded and followed Margaret into the kitchen.

"I feel like such a fool," Bess said.

Margaret busied herself with the preparations of making the tea. Her forehead was wrinkled with concentration.

"Jasmine?" Margaret said.

"I don't care. Will you please focus? Am I wrong? Do you think I did the wrong thing?"

Margaret watched the kettle as she waited for the steam to come curling from its spout. She turned to face Bess.

"I don't know."

"Really?"

Bess couldn't conceal her surprise—she had asked the question only because she had expected Margaret to assure her that she wasn't wrong.

"What's the big idea?" Margaret said. "I feel like we spend all our time talking about sex. If you love Lenny, why don't you sleep with him?"

They both stood watching the steam gain intensity.

"You sound like Sam," Bess said.

"Oh? You didn't mention anything about Sam."

It was Bess's turn to be reflective.

"Why don't we have the tea inside?" Bess said.

"I'd like to hear what Sam had to say."

Bess walked away.

The Manning living room was cluttered with "good" magazines and objets d'art. The disarray, so unlike her own home, appealed to Bess. There were so many things to distract her attention. She looked fondly at the collection of

27

glass miniatures scattered around the room, the ashtrays collected from restaurants and hotels, and the copies of *National Geographic, Smithsonian,* and *Vanity Fair.* Margaret's mother was a "subscription addict." Bess looked up when Margaret entered the room, carrying a lacquered tray. She carefully arranged everything on the coffee table and tore open a glassine bag of fortune cookies.

"Tea?" Margaret said.

"Who do you think you are? The damned queen of England?"

Margaret laughed and poured the tea. She picked up a fortune cookie and broke it in two.

"I don't want to hear it," Bess said.

"It's a good one."

"I don't want to hear it."

Margaret shrugged. "About Sam," she said.

"Oh, it's not such a big deal. He just said that there were plenty of girls who did sleep with guys, so why bother with a girl who wouldn't."

"In other words," Margaret said, "he took Lenny's side."

"You might say that."

Margaret crumbled the fortune cookie and played with the broken pieces.

"I'm surprised," Margaret said.

"Why?" Bess said. "He's a male, isn't he?"

"He's also your brother—your *older* brother."

"So?"

"Isn't he supposed to be a champion of your virginity? Shouldn't he have called Lenny a 'no good swine' or something equally chivalrous? After all, Lenny's goal was to destroy his sister's innocence."

"Come off it, Meg. It's not like that anymore."

"Exactly my point!" Margaret jumped up and started pacing excitedly around the room. "Nothing is the way it used to be. It just isn't any big deal to lose your virginity."

Bess started to laugh.

28

"You've been rehearsing too much for the part of Ophelia. I think you've snapped."

Margaret looked down at her, waving a finger.

"I'm right, and you know it. You're just too afraid to do anything about it."

Bess stood and glared at Margaret.

"Don't wave your finger at me," Bess said. "If you're so sure of yourself, why don't *you* volunteer your innocence to the highest bidder?"

They looked equally surprised—it had gone further than either of them had expected it to. They both giggled nervously and sprawled across the couch.

"I'm sorry," Margaret said. "I guess my timing was off."

"No, it's not that. You're right. I am making too much of the whole thing."

"Well, to you, it's a big thing."

Bess gave Margaret a long look.

"All right, all right," Margaret said. "I guess it's a big thing to me, too."

Bess put her hands behind her head and smiled fondly at Margaret.

"Let's talk about something *really* important," Bess said. "How am I going to face Lenny and the pom-pom queen at school tomorrow?"

"You just will," Margaret said. "You have no other choice."

"That sounds very ominous."

"Life, my dear," Margaret said, spreading her hands in front of her, "is very ominous, indeed."

"Thanks for the vote of confidence."

"My pleasure."

Bess checked her watch and started to rise.

"It's getting late. I'd better be going. I still have some homework to finish."

"Are you sure you'll be all right?"

"But of course."

29

Bess buttoned her coat, trying to avoid Margaret's concerned stare.

"Don't worry," Bess said. "I'll see you in school tomorrow."

She squeezed Margaret's arm with more confidence than she really felt. Margaret held the door open and watched Bess walk down the long hallway.

"I'll take the stairs," Bess said.

She raced down the stairs and into the cool night air, bending her head against the wind.

Bess didn't know why she was surprised. Margaret had told her that she had seen Lenny with Ellen Duncan in the hall between classes.

"I just wanted to prepare you," Margaret said.

"I've been trying to do just that myself," Bess said.

They hurried down the hall to their next class.

"I'm sorry about last night," Margaret said. "I wasn't being very sensitive."

"Forget it. I understand."

"I just wanted to tell you that you're allowed not to be ready. You know what I mean?"

Bess nodded, but she didn't really understand. How did you know when you were "ready"? Did a voice say "Now! This is the time!" She had waited to hear that voice tell her it was right with Lenny, but nothing had happened. She had made a terrible mistake. She had lost Lenny forever. There would never be anyone else.

She was so deeply involved with her thoughts that she didn't feel Margaret yank at her arm until it was too late. Bess practically walked right into Lenny and Ellen. They didn't see her—they were too busy with each other to notice anything else. Ellen was leaning against the lockers, looking up into Lenny's eyes. He was pressed against her— one hand protectively holding her waist and the other hand under her chin. It was straight out of a bad movie. Bess couldn't stop staring.

"C'mon," Margaret said. "Let's get outta here."

She tried to pull Bess away, but she was rooted to the ground. Ellen laughed and tilted her face up to meet Lenny's kiss. Bess gaped. Lenny had never been fond of public displays of affection, yet here he was practically on top of Ellen.

"Bess, let's go." Margaret's voice was persistent. It was too late. Lenny looked up and directly at Bess. Shock and embarrassment crossed his face. Ellen smiled coquettishly and linked her hand through Lenny's arm. Margaret was still holding on to Bess's sleeve, but now she shook herself free. The late bell rang, sending students hurrying in all directions.

"Let's go," Bess said. "We'll be late for class."

She smiled imperceptibly at Lenny and ignored Ellen. Without a backward glance at either of them, Bess marched off down the hall.

"Boy!" Margaret said. "You were terrific!"

Bess didn't feel terrific. In fact she worried all period that someone would hear the steady thumping of her heart.

Chapter 6

Bess waited anxiously in front of the girls' gym. If Margaret didn't show up soon, Bess decided she would leave.

"Bess!" Margaret said. She was racing down the hall. She looked flushed and excited.

"Where were you?" Bess said. "Why are you so late?"

Margaret's voice was breathless as she spoke.

"Sorry. C'mon, let's get changed. Are you all right?"

"I'm not going to gym," Bess said. "I have to go home. I don't feel well."

"Won't you get in trouble? At least go see the nurse."

"I'm not *that* kind of sick. I just feel funny."

"Do you want me to say anything to Ms. Stevens?"

"No. Don't bother."

Margaret looked reluctant to let Bess go.

"I'm sorry about before," Margaret said. "It must have been awful for you."

Bess swallowed hard to hold back her tears. She didn't want to start bawling right there in the middle of the hall. What if Lenny were to see her? Worse, what if Ellen saw her and told everyone in the school? Bess gulped and rubbed her eyes with her fist.

"I'm tired," Bess said. "I just need to sleep."

The halls were thinning out—students rushed to make their classes before the final bell.

"I'd better go," Margaret said. "I'll call you when I get home."

Bess smiled and nodded. She was puzzled by the hopeful look on Margaret's face—it wasn't until she was out of earshot that Bess remembered about the audition. How could she have forgotten? Now she felt even worse. There was no sense running after Margaret. She'd understand—Margaret was like that. Still, as she left the building, she couldn't stop thinking about how excited Margaret had looked as she came down the hall.

The bus stop was only two blocks from school. She saw the bus approaching just as she turned the corner, but she didn't run to catch it—she just didn't have the energy. Her arms and legs felt as if they were made of rubber. She felt achy. It wasn't as windy as it had been the last few days, and she decided to walk home. It wasn't more than thirty blocks, and she hoped the fresh air would make her feel better. After all, she had a lot of things to sort out. A girl just didn't lose her boyfriend *and* her dignity and come bobbing up to the surface that easily. There had to be some way of dealing with the pain.

The thirty blocks passed effortlessly. Bess checked her watch to see if her mother would be home yet. It would upset her to find that Bess had left school without permission. Nevertheless, when Bess unlocked the door and found the house silent, she was disappointed. Somewhere deep inside herself, she had really wanted her mother to be home. She would have pressed her cool hand against Bess's forehead and grazed her skin with her lips. Bess stood in the foyer of the apartment and felt lonelier than she had ever felt in her life. This time she didn't fight back the tears. She cried openly and deeply, pulling the tears from a place in her memory where tears were nothing to be ashamed of. A place where tears could soothe a nightmare, a scraped knee, a friend's broken promise, or the loss of a toy. Standing there, her fists clenched and chest heaving, she felt caught between the past and the future. Images flashed through her mind—Lenny taking her hand for the first time, shyly reaching to kiss her and laughing when their noses bumped. It seemed inconceivable to her that she would never share such moments with him again and even more impossible to believe that she would ever share them with someone else. It was her first real loss—her first experience with separation. The pain was unbearable.

She stretched out across the couch and fell asleep. When she awoke, it felt as if she had slept for hours. The grumbling in her stomach signaled her that it was past lunchtime. She was very hungry.

It was still too early for Margaret to be home. She fixed herself a huge bologna and cheese sandwich. She took great hungry bites as she stared at the kitchen clock. She was eager to speak to Margaret. When the phone rang, she practically jumped out of her seat.

"Bess?"

Margaret didn't even wait for her to say hello.

"Margaret? Are you all right? Where are you?"

"I'm still at school. I saw Lenny. He was very upset. I think he's on the way to your house. I wanted to warn you."

Bess started pacing nervously.

"He's coming here? What does he want? What did you tell him?"

"I told him I didn't think you'd want to see him, but he wouldn't listen. He said something about 'getting things straight.' Do you want me to come over?"

Bess tried to think. Her head was spinning. What would she say to Lenny?

"Did you get the part?" Bess said.

"What?"

"Did you get your part. You know, Ophelia. Did you get it?"

Margaret started laughing.

34

"Is this what you call a delayed reaction?" she said.

"I guess. Well, did you?"

"I think so. I'll know for sure on Wednesday. Do you want me to come over?"

"No. I'm glad about the audition. Don't worry about me. Let me go. I'll call you later."

"Bess, one more thing."

"What?"

"I'm glad you remembered."

"I'm glad I did, too."

Bess hung up the phone and raced into the bathroom. She splashed her face with cool water and brushed her hair. Maybe they could work things out. Maybe everything would be all right. Ellen wasn't for Lenny. Just as she was deciding if she should change, the doorbell rang. Lenny was leaning against the doorjamb, breathing heavily.

"Don't you ask who it is before you open the door?" he said.

"I was expecting you."

"Margaret called. I thought she would."

"I could have said I had a premonition." Bess hoped she would make Lenny smile—it didn't work.

"Can I come in?" he said.

Bess extended her arm and allowed Lenny to pass.

"By all means," she said. "What are *friends* for?"

Lenny missed her sarcasm and headed straight for the kitchen. Bess told herself to calm down. Why was she acting like such a jerk? She'd never win him back by being nasty. Still, she refused to ask him if he was hungry. There was a limit to her generosity. Cool and casual, that's how she would play it.

"So, what do you want?" Bess said.

"What do you have?"

Bess realized that he thought she was asking him about something to eat. She started to giggle.

"What's so goddamn funny?" Lenny said.

"You."

35

"Oh, yeah?"

"Brilliant comeback, Len. I'm really impressed."

She could tell he was really angry—the tips of his ears were bright red.

"I ask you a simple question, and you give me a nasty answer," Lenny said. "I practically killed myself getting here because I was so worried about you."

Bess's fantasy about "working things out" burst. She saw it fizzle as it would in a cartoon, slithering down in a blur of colors. She was furious.

"You pompous ass!" she said. "You walk in here with your smug concern for me and expect to be fed. I wanted to know what you wanted from me, not what you wanted to eat!"

Lenny's expression softened.

"I'm sorry," he said. "I feel like a jerk. Old habits are hard to break."

Bess started crying again.

"I can't believe I'm crying again," she said. She stamped her foot. "I've been crying all day. You know how much I hate to cry."

Lenny stood and reached to comfort her.

"Leave me alone," she said. Her voice didn't sound very convincing.

She was moved by the concern in his face. She didn't resist him when he bent down to kiss her. In fact, she returned his kisses with equal energy. She suddenly realized that Lenny might take her behavior as a cue that she had changed her mind. She hadn't. She knew that. She pulled away from him.

"What's the matter?" he said.

"Everything," Bess said. "Nothing's changed."

"I don't understand."

"I'm just not ready for all this.'

"For kissing?"

"You know what I mean. You know why we broke up— or rather, why *you* broke up with me."

36

"Ellen's just a girl. It's not the same. You must know that."

Something about his words made her realize what had been really bothering her—Lenny. He didn't care about Ellen at all.

"You don't really care about Ellen," she said. "Do you?"

"She's okay. She's just a girl. You know what I mean?"

She looked directly at him, although he tried to avoid her eyes.

"I don't know," she said. "I think you should go."

"What are you talking about?"

"I want you to leave. I really do."

"I don't understand you," Lenny said. "What are you trying to do?"

Bess thought for a minute before answering.

"I guess I'm trying to find my own way," she said. "Just like you."

Lenny shifted uncomfortably in his seat.

"Sometimes people get hurt," Bess said, more to herself than to Lenny. "I'm sorry that this time it was you."

Lenny brightened and stood up. He made a move toward her, but she pressed her hand flat against his chest.

"Let me finish," she said. "I'm sorry it was you this time, but I'm glad it wasn't me."

After Lenny left, Bess leaned her head against the door and smiled. It hadn't turned out to be such a rotten day after all.

Chapter 7

Margaret felt better after her conversation with Bess. At least Bess had remembered to ask her how the audition had been. Lately Margaret felt as if Bess's problems were taking over her life. It had always been that way, and Margaret was beginning to resent it. It wasn't just Bess's problems—Margaret knew it was hard for her to talk about her own difficulties. Why didn't Bess ever have that trouble?

Pushing her way out of the big double doors at the school's main entrance, Margaret studied the faces of the girls and boys she saw every day. Most of them were laughing and shoving one another. The good-looking kids were all paired off. You could tell the popular kids from those who just sort of plodded along—they walked alone or in groups of two or three. They didn't hurry down to the local hangouts to talk about whatever it was they talked about. Margaret couldn't be sure because she had never been part of any group. She had had her chance. Just knowing Bess would have made Margaret's presence acceptable. Still, Margaret had always begged off. She had drama rehearsals or part-time jobs. Baby-sitting for Janie was *always* a convenient excuse. It was only recently that

Margaret was feeling as if she had missed something along the way.

"Hey, Margaret! Wait up!"

Margaret turned around. It was Nora Siegel—another one of the school misfits. She still wore the same kind of glasses she had been wearing since the fifth grade. Margaret wondered if they were the same pair. Her head *must* have grown.

"Hi, Nora."

"Are you going home?" Nora said. "We could take the bus together."

Margaret frantically searched for an excuse, but her mind was blank. The last thing in the world she felt like doing was riding the bus with Nora chewing her ear off.

"Where's Bess?" Nora said. "I saw her in history this morning, but she wasn't in math. Is she sick? I didn't see her name on the early dismissal list. I work in the main office during my study period, so I would have seen her name."

Margaret was amazed by Nora's recitation—it seemed as if she hadn't even taken a breath.

"How have you been?" Margaret said. "I hardly ever see you."

Margaret was stalling for time, and she hoped her question would get Nora off the subject of Bess. Whenever Margaret was alone, someone was bound to ask "Where's Bess?" Margaret wondered now if anyone ever asked Bess "Where's Margaret?" She doubted it.

"I saw Lenny in the hall with Ellen Duncan," Nora said. "I thought Bess and Lenny were inseparable."

"They had an operation," Margaret said. "It's a milestone in adolescent surgery. Didn't you read about it in the *Enquirer*?"

Nora made a face. It made her look even less attractive than any one person should be. Margaret was surprised that she didn't even feel sorry for Nora.

"You don't have to be so nasty," Nora said. "I was just asking."

The wind blew strands of Margaret's hair into her face. She pressed one hand down on her skirt to keep it from flying up. Pretty soon it would be time for winter coats. Margaret waited for the encounter with Nora to end. Margaret didn't want to be the one to end it. Nora was an easy target for Margaret's lousy mood.

"I guess I'd better be going," Nora said. "It's getting cold."

Margaret nodded and watched Nora walk away. Who did she think she was asking questions about Bess? Margaret waited until Nora was safely out of sight before heading in the same direction.

"I thought we'd never be alone."

Margaret looked over her shoulder to see Zak walking behind her. His red hair looked even redder than her imagination would have allowed her to recall. It was the boldest statement she could ever remember hearing him make.

"Zak," Margaret said. "Have you been following me?"

Zak blushed, and his hair seemed to turn a deeper shade of red. He must have a million freckles.

"Not exactly," Zak said. "I was waiting for you to finish your conversation with Nora. I didn't want to interrupt."

"Next time you see me with Nora, don't be so polite."

Zak laughed and matched his stride to Margaret's.

"I saw your audition today," he said. "You were very good."

"Just 'very good'?" Margaret said. "Not brilliant or spectacular?"

Zak seemed to give that serious thought.

"I generally hesitate to use such extravagant adjectives," he said. "They have a tendency to obscure reality. Still, I would be comfortable with 'excellent' and the potential to become either 'brilliant' or 'spectacular.'"

It was Margaret's turn to laugh. She was instantly sorry. Zak hadn't been trying to be funny.

"I'm sorry," Margaret said. "I wasn't really laughing at you. It's just that you seemed so serious."

"I was serious," Zak said.

"I know. Well, now I know. I didn't know when I laughed."

Zak raised his right hand and stopped walking.

"Slow down," he said. "I accept your apology."

Margaret smiled and felt suddenly shy. He was a very strange boy. He really wasn't bad-looking. His nose was a little pointy, and his hair was impossibly red. Still, he had beautiful green eyes. Margaret didn't think she had ever seen anyone with such green eyes. What color eyes did Sam have? Brown? No, she thought, they were more grayish.

"Thanks for the rave review," Margaret said. "I hope Mr. Rand feels as strongly about my audition as you do."

"He does," Zak said. "Rest assured."

"How do you know?"

"I could tell from his expression. He had an incomparable look of smug satisfaction plastered all over his usually dour face."

Margaret giggled and reached for Zak's arm simultaneously—it was a purely spontaneous action. Zak seemed to stop breathing as soon as Margaret's hand made contact with his jacket.

"God," she said. "What a great description of him. It's perfect."

"I have a gift for characterization," Zak said. His voice was very soft.

"What were you doing there, anyway?" Margaret said. "Are you trying out for a part?"

They had started walking again. Zak was intently studying the cracks in the pavement. Margaret was briefly reminded of the silly childhood rhyme, "Step on a crack, break your mother's back." The memory warmed her.

"I came to watch you," Zak said.

41

"Me? Why?"

"I wanted to," Zak said. "Anyway, I love the theater."

"I wouldn't exactly call a school play the theater," Margaret said. "I'm flattered that you came."

"Well, I'm writing a piece for the school paper, and I wanted to cover the auditions."

"Oh."

Margaret felt vaguely disappointed. She had forgotten that Zak was the editor of the school paper, *The Westside Watchdog*. The title had always reminded her of a vigilante group rather than a school paper. She suppressed the urge to make a clever remark about her observation. There was no sense in putting Zak on the spot just because she had an evil streak in her.

"I'm really glad I was there," Zak said. "Even if I didn't have to come."

Margaret accepted his peace offering in the spirit it was given. She suddenly realized that she had walked past her bus stop.

"Damn it!" she said. "I walked blocks out of my way. I should have turned three blocks back."

"I'm sorry," Zak said. "I should have been paying attention."

Margaret looked confused.

"How would you have known?"

Zak looked startled and tried to accomodate for his error. "I mean, we were so busy talking that I probably distracted you. I should have reminded you to check."

"You didn't distract me."

"I didn't?"

"Well," Margaret said. "I was enjoying our conversation, but I didn't feel distracted."

"Are we going to argue semantics?" Zak said.

He smiled. Margaret thought it was more of a grin, so she grinned back.

"I'm going to have to carry a dictionary when I talk to you."

42

"I hope you'll be needing one."

They stood facing each other, smiling shyly but happily.

"You know where I live," Margaret said. "Don't you?"

"I plead the Fifth," Zak said. "I won't talk until I contact my lawyer."

"Very sensible of you."

The sun had dropped out of sight behind the clouds, and the air felt raw. Zak shoved his hands deep into his pockets and kicked at the pavement. Margaret was relieved to note that he wasn't wearing white socks—she hated white socks. It was just a thing she had.

"Do you have to go right home?" Zak said. "Do you have time for some hot chocolate or something?"

"The 'or something' sounds particularly appealing," Margaret said.

"There's a place on the next corner," Zak said. "They make great 'or somethings,' and even better hot chocolate."

"Let's go. I'm freezing."

They talked without stopping all the way to the coffee shop and all through two cups of hot chocolate. It wasn't until they were walking back out into the chill dusk that Margaret remembered she had promised Bess to call her the minute she got home.

Chapter 8

Bess let the phone ring at least twenty times before hanging up. She couldn't understand why Margaret wasn't home. She checked the kitchen clock once again and tried to remember if Margaret had said she was stopping off somewhere after school. Carefully, Bess reviewed their earlier hasty conversation—she was certain Margaret had said she was going directly home and would call immediately. Stubbornly, Bess dialed the number she knew as well as her own and imagined the red wall phone in Margaret's kitchen demanding to be answered. Why didn't she answer? It was awfully quiet in Bess's own kitchen, and she wondered if she could be the last person left in the world. She shivered and hugged herself. She really knew how to give herself the creeps. When the key suddenly turned in the front door, she started with a pounding heart.

"Anybody home? I could use a hand."

Her mother's breathless voice filled the emptiness with welcomed life.

"Coming!" Bess said.

Her mother was trying to hold the front door open with one foot while negotiating several bursting grocery bags and two boxes displaying the logo of a fancy local boutique.

"I'm glad to see you," her mother said. Her cheeks were flushed, and several strands of her dark hair fell into her face, making her look attractively girlish. "Can you believe I stopped for one thing?"

Bess giggled and hoisted two grocery bags in her arms. On her way to the kitchen she called over her shoulder, "You always say that."

Her mother followed close at Bess's heels.

"You'd think they were giving something away," her mother said. "You should have seen how packed the market was. Tuna fish was ninety-nine cents a can, but they had a six-can limit. I stopped at the butcher and bought some steaks. Your father and I could have eaten for two weeks for what three steaks cost today."

Bess poured herself a glass of milk while her mother shook her head in disbelief. She looked around the room for the boxes her mother had been carrying. They were nowhere to be found.

"What happened to the two boxes?" Bess said.

Her mother continued putting away the groceries. Her face wore a look of deep concentration that didn't at all suit the task—she could have found her way around the kitchen blindfolded.

"I thought I had tomato paste," she said. "I'm always forgetting something. This time I forgot my list and remembered the coupons. I don't know what's happening to me."

She kept her back to Bess during the mindless chatter.

"Mom, what happened to the boxes? You had them when you came in."

Her mother turned to face Bess but avoided meeting her eyes. Her cheeks seemed to be more flushed than they were when she'd first walked in the door. Bess thought how pretty her mother was.

"Honey," her mother said. "could you see if you could find some tomato paste? I'm sure I had some."

Bess couldn't figure out what her mother was being so

45

mysterious about. Whatever was in those boxes, she obviously didn't want Bess to know about it. They couldn't be birthday gifts—her birthday wasn't until December, and her mother was the classic last-minute shopper. Bess decided to drop her inquiry. At least now her mother would know what it was like to be pressured about something you didn't feel like talking about. Funny how different it was when the shoe was on the other foot. She rummaged through the cabinets in search of tomato paste and tried to stop thinking about the contents of the boxes.

"Is one can enough?" Bess said. "That's all I can find."

"It'll have to do," her mother said. "I'll put it on my list—I'm sure to remember it next time."

They maintained an awkward silence. Sooner or later she would have to tell her mother about Lenny. Neither of her parents knew that they had broken up. She wondered what their reaction would be. They were both quite fond of Lenny.

"Can I help with anything?" Bess said.

Her mother turned to her and smiled—this time she didn't avoid her eyes.

"Thank you, yes. Why don't you start the salad. I bought some lovely fresh vegetables at the Korean market. Be sure to toss in some pignoli nuts. I feel celebratory tonight."

"Oh?" Bess tried to think of what could possibly be making her mother act so silly. Could she be having an affair? Impossible! Her mother was much too straight for *that*.

"I'm just going to change out of these clothes," her mother said. "I'll be back in a jiffy."

Bess cringed. Occasionally, her mother used words like *jiffy, goody,* or *yummy.* It drove her crazy, but there was no point in saying anything. Her mother thought she over-reacted to everything.

Actually her mother did return in a "jiffy," wearing a pair of old slacks and a sweatshirt that Sam had left behind.

"So," her mother said. "What's new with you? We haven't had a chance to talk in ages."

"In ages" was another one of those expressions that Bess and Margaret liked to use when they were imitating their mothers. Bess smiled and started tearing up the lettuce into bite-sized pieces. Her mother had dumped ground beef into the mixing bowl and was breaking it up with her fingers. "The only way to make good meat loaf," she always said, "is to use your hands."

"Nothing much," Bess said. "Well, that's not really true."

"What's that supposed to mean?" her mother said.

Bess cursed herself for initiating the discussion. She didn't really feel like talking about Lenny. She wished Margaret would hurry up and call.

"You don't have to talk about it if you don't want to," her mother said.

Suddenly talking was exactly what Bess felt like doing. She remembered how disappointed she had been not to find her mother home earlier in the day. After all, her mother had been young once, too.

"No," Bess said. "I really do feel like talking about it. I just don't know where to begin."

"I suggest you take a deep breath and start anyplace that feels comfortable."

Bess turned the cold tap water on and let it run over the lettuce. She liked the way the drops of water clung to its oily surface. She knelt down to get the salad spinner from the cupboard. Her mother was extremely fond of kitchen gadgets. They were probably the only people on the West Side with a strawberry huller. She inhaled theatrically and spurt out a loud breath.

"Lenny and I broke up. To be more accurate, Lenny broke up with me."

Her mother stopped mixing the meat and looked momentarily wistful. Bess wasn't sure why, but her attention was fixed on the tiny bits of bright red meat that clung to her mother's fingers. It was a grisly sight.

"Oh, Bess. I'm so sorry. When did this happen?"

"I guess it's been happening for a while. Officially we parted the other night."

Her mother started viciously pummeling the meat with one hand while reaching for the container of bread crumbs with the other. "Could you hand me an egg?" she said. "I thought you looked sort of funny. I even said something to your father. He told me I was imagining things. Men!"

Bess gave her an egg and tried not to laugh. She didn't think people really said things like "men" anymore. Bess felt very tender toward her mother—she was really a very nice person.

"I know that you mean," Bess said.

"Was there a specific reason?" her mother said.

Bess wanted to talk about it like an adult, but it would be embarrassing. She had never really talked to her mother about sex. She remembered the conversation they had had about menstruation. They had both been so serious as her mother had demonstrated on one of Bess's dolls the proper way to wear a sanitary belt and pad. Bess had been the one to introduce her mother to tampons.

It seemed like a good time to take another deep breath and plunge ahead.

"I wouldn't sleep with him," she said. She waited for her mother's response, but none came. "Mom?"

Her mother walked over to the sink and ran the water. She squirted some Ivory liquid from the container and methodically washed her hands. As she dried her hands on a piece of paper towel, she seemed to be mustering her courage to utter the one-syllable word that would open many doors.

"Why?"

Bess hadn't been prepared for this question.

" 'Why?' " she repeated.

"That's what I said," her mother said. She smiled. "Why don't we sit down for a few minutes? Your father won't be home for quite a while."

Bess took a seat across from her mother at the kitchen table.

"Would you like some coffee?" her mother said.

Bess shook her head. Nervously she started fidgeting with the tablecloth.

"Are you shocked?" she said.

"Shocked? No, I don't think so," her mother said. "I knew it was bound to come up sooner or later. I guess I was hoping for a bit later. I can't say I haven't worried about it. We should have talked about this sooner."

"That's all right."

Her mother reached across the table and took Bess's hand in her own.

"It must have been very difficult for you to say no to Lenny."

Bess's eyes filled with tears. She drew in her breath sharply and hung her head down. She didn't want to cry.

"Are you sorry?" her mother said.

"I was until this afternoon," Bess said. "I'm not anymore."

"What changed your mind?"

"Lenny."

"I don't understand."

"Oh, Mom. It's a long story. Lenny's started seeing this girl, Ellen Duncan. I saw them together in the hall today. I was really upset. I guess I was upset at her. You know, I felt as if it was all her fault."

Her mother nodded and continued holding her hand.

"Well, Lenny came over after school today. I realized that he doesn't really care about Ellen. He just got tired of waiting for me. It really bothered me. I expected more from him."

Her mother withdrew her hand and folded her arms across her chest.

"I wouldn't want to be a teenager today," she said. "It's much too complicated." She sighed.

"It shouldn't be," Bess said.

"You still didn't answer my question. Why didn't you sleep with Lenny?"

"It just didn't feel right. I don't know. My instincts told me he wasn't the one."

"If you'd thought it was the right time," her mother said, "would you have slept with him?"

"I guess so."

"You're still *very* young. Too young, I think. Don't push yourself. I'm not saying to do things as we did them when I was your age, but I am telling you that having sex because everyone else is can only hurt you."

"I know that."

"I know you know that. I had to tell you anyway."

They laughed companionably.

"Were you a virgin when you married Dad?"

"I'm almost ashamed to say yes. Still, I have no choice. Yes, I was a virgin."

"Was Dad?"

Her mother looked startled.

"What a marvelously contemporary question!" she said. "No one in my years would ever have thought to ask such a question."

"Well, was he?"

"*That's* something you'll have to ask your father."

"I don't think I'm *that* modern!"

"Well, at least some things haven't changed."

They looked at each other fondly. Bess felt extremely close to her mother, closer than she could ever remember feeling.

"Mom, what would you have said if I had told you that I had slept with Lenny?"

Her mother stood and went to turn on the oven. It was a ploy to give her a few seconds to think. She peered at the numbers on the dial and seemed to have nothing on her mind other than whether to set the oven at three-fifty or four hundred.

"Mom?"

"I'm stalling. Give me a few seconds."

"Okay."

Her mother walked back to the table and looked down at Bess.

"I'd like to be able to tell you that I would ask you about birth control, but it's not true. I'd be concerned about your emotional involvement. Mostly, I'd be worried that you'd get hurt."

Bess looked up at her mother.

"Well, you don't have to worry," Bess said.

"Not yet, anyway," her mother said.

Neither of them spoke for a few moments as they pondered how soon in the future "yet" would be. Suddenly her mother broke the silence.

"Do you want to see what I bought today?" she said.

Bess had forgotten about the two boxes.

"I'd love to."

Her mother disappeared and returned, holding the boxes.

"It's our anniversary next week," she said. "Twenty-three years. It doesn't seem possible, but it's true. Anyway, your father and I are going to spend the weekend at the Waldorf-Astoria!"

"Dad didn't tell me! How exciting. What a romantic idea."

Her mother laughed and started tugging at the ribbon on the box.

"Dad didn't tell you because he doesn't know. It's a surprise. I have the reservations. I even bought the clothes to go with the weekend."

Carefully she pulled aside the tissue paper and held up a beautiful lavender peignoir set.

"Oh!" Bess said. "It's magnificent. You'll look gorgeous in it!"

"Look what I bought Dad." She opened the other box and took out a royal blue velvet smoking jacket. "Your father has always wanted one like this."

"It's great. You'll both look terrific."

"Pretty classy, don't you think? I hope the Waldorf is ready for us."

Bess reached over and kissed her mother on the cheek.

"I don't think the Waldorf-Astoria is classy enough for you," she said.

Her mother smiled appreciatively. They both jumped when they heard the front door open. Bess helped her mother close the boxes.

"Where are my gorgeous women?" her father shouted as he slammed the door behind him.

"Quick!" her mother said. "Hide the boxes! I'll stall him."

Bess grabbed the boxes and ran out of the kitchen toward her bedroom. Out of the corner of her eye, she saw her mother embracing her father in the doorway. She was waving her hand behind her back at Bess.

She quietly closed the door to her room and hid the boxes beneath her bed. She gave her parents a few more seconds to finish their greeting. It occurred to Bess that if she were very lucky, someday she might have someone to take away for a romantic weekend.

Chapter 9

Almost a week had passed since Margaret had taken her first walk with Zak. Bess had pressed her for details, but Margaret had been reluctant to discuss her feelings. Zak was nice, but he wasn't Sam. How could she possibly explain that to Bess? She was still very moody over her breakup with Lenny. Frankly, Margaret was losing patience with her. There were too many things going on in Margaret's own life these days to be preoccupied with Bess's melancholy. Bess was still angry at her for not calling that afternoon she had walked home from school with Zak. Big deal! Was that a reason to stay angry for so long? Margaret tried to concentrate on her lines. Rehearsals started tomorrow, and she still hadn't memorized her part. Mr. Rand would have a fit. Bess had even been cool about Margaret's victory in landing the role of Ophelia in the school play. She seemed to think the whole world revolved around her.

In spite of her annoyance with Bess's attitude, Margaret couldn't help but feel bad about the way things had been going. It must be really rough on Bess having to see Lenny and Ellen at school every day. They had become something of an item—probably because Lenny and Bess had practically been a national monument. It seemed as if Lenny and Ellen did nothing but neck. One of them was always pressed up against a locker with the other one doing *a lot* of heavy leaning. Personally Margaret found it pretty crude. Furthermore, it just didn't seem like Lenny at all. Amazing what sex could do to a person. She had seen Zak two or three times this week already. Once they had gone to a movie. He had tentatively draped an arm across her shoulder and squeezed her. When he turned her face toward his for a kiss, she hadn't resisted. His mouth had tasted pleasantly of Reese's Peanut Butter Cups—one of her favorites. They had held hands walking home, and he had kissed her goodnight. So far, things were still pretty tame. Margaret wasn't sure how far she was willing to let things go.

Suddenly Margaret had an irresistible urge to speak to Bess. There was no sense in letting this go on forever. They were still best friends. She dialed Bess's number and was just about to hang up when Bess's sleepy voice answered. Margaret hadn't realized how early it still was—Bess was a late sleeper.

"Hello?"

"Bess Harriet Ellis?" Margaret said, disguising her voice.

No one, but no one, knew Bess's middle name. Margaret was sure that even the F.B.I. would have a hard time getting that information.

"Huh?" Bess said.

"Is this Bess Harriet Ellis?" Margaret said.

"Who is this?"

"Do I have the right party?"

"This is Bess Ellis. Who are you?"

Margaret put her hand over the phone because she couldn't help giggling.

"I represent a major radio station. Your name has been selected from thousands of others for a fabulous weekend for two at the beautiful Three Mile Island!"

"I didn't enter a contest," Bess said. "How did you get my name?"

Margaret tried to control herself—Bess was so damned logical.

"Isn't Three Mile Island a nuclear plant?" Bess said. "Why would anyone want to go there? Who is this, anyway?"

Margaret gave up. Bess was the worst when it came to jokes—she always asked so many questions that you were sorry you had told her the joke in the first place. Margaret felt foolish. She should never have called.

"It's me, Bess," she said. "I guess my joke wasn't very funny."

"Margaret? What the hell is wrong with you? It's eight-thirty on a Sunday morning. Why aren't you sleeping?"

"I wanted to talk."

"What was all that nonsense about Three Mile Island?"

"A joke—at least *I* thought it was funny."

Bess sighed.

"Could you hold on a second? I have to put some water on my face. I'm still half asleep."

Margaret heard Bess closing a door. With the phone pressed close to her ear, she waited patiently for Bess to return.

"I'm back," Bess said. "What's up?"

"I wanted to talk," Margaret repeated. "About us."

"What about us?"

There were the questions again. It was enough to make anyone crazy.

"I wanted to talk about the way we haven't been talking," Margaret said.

"Okay."

Margaret was so relieved that Bess didn't pursue the issue that she started babbling.

"Why don't we meet for breakfast? There's a real cute new place on Columbus Avenue that just opened a few weeks ago. I heard they squeeze fresh orange juice. I'll treat. What do you think?"

"Sounds great."

"Terrific! When can you meet me?"

"Well, I have to shower and get dressed. How about in an hour? I'll pack later."

"Pack?" Margaret said.

"For my fabulous weekend at Three Mile Island!"

Margaret laughed. She was feeling better already. She gave Bess the name and address of the restaurant and hung up the phone.

It was still too early for the restaurant to be crowded. Margaret arrived before Bess and asked for a table near the window. It was a warm morning for November—Thanksgiving would be here soon. Sam would certainly be coming home for the holidays.

"Coffee?" The waitress stood over Margaret with a steaming pot.

"Sure," Margaret said. She smiled.

"Can I get you anything else?"

"No, thanks. I'm waiting for someone. I'll order then."

Margaret studied the passersby from her window seat. Everyone was either walking a dog or dragging a copy of the *New York Times* under one arm and a bag of breakfast supplies in the other. Almost everyone looked sleepy and disheveled. She sipped her coffee and searched the passing faces for Bess's. Suddenly Margaret spotted her across the street. She was turning her head in either direction to determine if it was safe to cross against the light. There wasn't a car in sight. Margaret looked enviously at Bess's leggy strides. She walked with complete confidence. Her dark hair gleamed in the morning sunlight. Margaret couldn't see her eyes behind the dark sunglasses, but she knew their shape and color from memory—almond-shaped and gray. Her hands were stuffed in the pockets of her down vest and a bright red scarf dangled around her neck. The only jewelry she wore was a pair of tiny gold hoops that she had been wearing since she had had her ears pierced in the seventh grade.

Margaret rapped lightly on the window, but she knew it was impossible for Bess to hear from that distance. She continued to rap anyway, eager to make contact. Bess dashed across the street as a lone taxi hurled down the empty avenue. This time Bess saw Margaret and smiled. Margaret watched as Bess came through the door and pointed in her direction as the waitress approached. For some silly reason, Margaret felt as if she should rise when Bess reached the table. Instead, she formally bowed her head.

"Good morning," Margaret said.

Bess took her seat and immediately took off her vest. She was wearing a bulky Mexican sweater, which she also removed to reveal a white turtleneck—it was a wonderful contrast against her dark skin.

"What are you dressed for?" Margaret said. "The blizzard of the century?"

"I was cold," Bess said. "I just stepped out of the shower."

"Do you want coffee?"

Bess nodded. Margaret signaled the waitress.

"What are you going to have?" Bess said.

"Just some grapefruit and whole wheat toast. Maybe an egg."

Bess smiled.

"Will it bother you if I gorge?" she said.

Margaret was used to Bess's enormous appetite. She hardly ever seemed to gain a pound. It was just one of life's injustices.

"Be my guest."

Bess studied the menu with deep concentration.

"They have fresh fruit salad," she said. "Maybe you could have that with some cottage cheese."

"Sounds good."

Bess put down the menu and cleared her throat.

"There's something I've been wanting to tell you all week."

"Oh?" Margaret couldn't help but be surprised—it wasn't like Bess to hold *anything* back.

"Is it serious?" Margaret said.

"I think so."

Margaret's heart started pounding—Sam's getting married. She was sure of it.

"You look absolutely gorgeous," Bess said. "I mean it."

Margaret felt her face flush with pleasure. She had lost eight pounds, but she hadn't thought anyone had noticed.

"I've been meaning to tell you, but things sort of got in the way."

"That's okay. I lost eight pounds."

"It looks like more. Your face looks so different."

"Tell me more," Margaret said. "I love it!"

The waitress approached with coffee. She took their orders after assuring Margaret that the salad was made entirely of fresh fruit.

Bess was right. Much of the roundness had left Margaret's normally full cheeks. Her blue eyes appeared more prominent, and her chin jutted forward proudly, no longer hidden by a layer of fleshiness.

"You look different," Bess said. "I don't know how to explain it."

"Try."

Bess sipped at her coffee and scrutinized Margaret's face, trying to find in it the words she needed to explain what she saw.

"You look older. You don't look cute anymore."

"I don't?"

"Let me finish—you look sexy."

Margaret opened her mouth in surprise.

"Really?" she said. "You really think I look sexy?"

A few people in the restaurant turned around to stare at them. Margaret's voice had risen an octave higher than its normal range.

"Shh!" Bess said. "The whole place is looking at us."

"I don't care. They probably all want to see this sexy broad."

They both giggled and bent their heads toward each other.

"I'm glad you came," Margaret said.

"Why wouldn't I?"

Margaret fidgeted uncomfortably and toyed with her napkin.

"It's been kind of a lousy week," she said. "I guess I haven't been paying much attention to you."

Bess tilted her coffee cup and stared at the murky brown liquid—Margaret still couldn't figure out how she drank her coffee black. She had finally learned how to do without sugar, but she needed a little milk.

"I've been pretty busy with my own feelings these days," Bess said. "I haven't really been a very good friend to you."

"Don't say that!"

"Why not? It's true. It's really my fault."

Margaret laughed and shook her head.

"God! We sound like something out of a soap opera. 'It's my fault. No! No! It's my fault!' she said with a toss of her raven hair. Really, Bess, we've got to stop this. We're making me sick."

Bess reached across the table and gave Margaret a tentative shove.

"Okay. Let's forget the whole thing. Tell me about the play."

Margaret's face lit up.

"It's wonderful! I've never been so excited about doing a part in my life. I should be home right now studying, but I'll do it later. It's just very exciting. It's a very challenging role. I'm really getting into going mad." She made a horrible face and rolled her eyes.

"Stop it!" Bess shrieked. "You look awful!"

"Thank you."

The waitress arrived with their orders and looked strangely at Margaret.

"I'm practicing going crazy," she said.

"Get a job here," the waitress said. "I promise you, it'll be all the practice you need."

Bess snickered behind her hand.

"Will that be all?" the waitress said.

Both girls nodded.

"Why do you always want to shock people?" Bess said.

"It's a hobby," Margaret said. She thrust her fork into the mound of cottage cheese and speared a grapefruit section.

Bess meticulously inserted pats of butter between her pancakes and drowned the stack in maple syrup. She eyed the sausages suspiciously.

"I should have ordered bacon," she said.

"Could we talk about something else besides food?" Margaret said. "Tell me more about how sexy I look."

"Hasn't Zak told you?"

Margaret turned her head to look out the window. She didn't really feel like talking about Zak, but there didn't seem to be any way out of it.

"Let's talk about food," she said.

"Make up your mind."

"It's just hard for me. I don't really know what to say. He's nice—that's about it."

Bess chewed her food slowly and delicately wiped the corners of her mouth. She was the slowest eater Margaret had ever seen.

"What does 'nice' mean?" Bess said. "He hasn't attacked you yet?"

"What does 'attack' mean? If you mean, has he thrown me down and ravished my milky white skin? Well, the answer to that is no. If you mean, has he kissed me and tentatively touched me in certain strategic locations? Well, the answer to that is yes. Are you satisfied?"

"I guess."

Neither of them said anything for a few moments,

pretending to be deeply engrossed in their eating. Margaret wondered how strawberries would taste dipped in maple syrup, but she restrained herself from trying.

"I didn't mean to be nasty," Margaret said. "I told you I didn't know what to say. It's not what you think. I like Zak, but he doesn't send my heart racing the way . . ."

"The way Sam does?" Bess said.

Margaret tried not to look startled by Bess's bluntness, but there was nothing she could do about the steady blush she felt creeping up her neck. She wasn't going to say that at all—not that she wasn't thinking it, but she would *never* say it.

"I was going to say, the way Lenny made you feel."

Margaret hated herself the minute the words were out of her mouth. It really was what she was going to say, but she had checked herself out of sensitivity for Bess's feelings. Still, if Bess could be so insensitive, she didn't have to be careful about her choice of words.

"Touché," Bess said. "I guess I deserved that."

Margaret pushed her plate away and reached across the table to touch Bess's arm. What was happening to them? They had never been like this before. Margaret felt petty and mean. The feelings frightened and confused her. Both she and Bess had always shielded each other from all the small hurts that others seemed to inflict on one another. Wasn't that what best friends were for? Even now, reaching to touch Bess's arm, Margaret felt cautious about intruding. The feelings were new and disturbing. Bess didn't resist her touch but smiled wanly at Margaret.

"What's happening to us?" Margaret said. "I don't understand. I feel so weird."

Bess shrugged and held her palms face-up. Her expression reflected consternation equal to Margaret's

"Could we still be going through puberty?" Bess said.

Margaret laughed, somewhat relieved. At least they could still laugh about things. That was a small comfort.

"I could use a hot fudge sundae," Margaret said. "I feel a crisis coming on."

"Don't you dare! You've worked so hard, and you look so terrific."

"I think I'm getting back into the swing of this conversation."

"We're still not talking about it," Bess said.

"God, that 'it' sounds so ominous. Hey," Margaret said suddenly, "do you feel like walking? This place isn't as hot as I thought it would be." She felt excited about the prospect of moving, getting out. "Let's get outta here. What do you think?"

Bess also seemed to brighten. "Good idea. I'll get the check."

"I'm paying. I said I would."

Bess took a final sip of coffee. "Fine," she said. "I'll just stop at the ladies' room. I'll meet you outside."

Margaret left a ridiculously large tip, hoping to insure the success of the rest of the morning.

Neither of the girls suggested a direction in which to walk—they both naturally headed for the park. It was where they always walked, and where they always did some of their best talking. They walked in step, with heads bent. Bess hummed softly to herself, and Margaret eagerly picked up the tune and accompanied her.

"What's that from?" Margaret said.

"I'm not sure, but it keeps playing over and over in my head."

Margaret slipped her hand through Bess's arm and began chanting, "LEFT, LEFT, left my wife with forty-eight kids on the verge of starvation without any gingerbread just because I thought it was RIGHT, RIGHT, right in the middle of the kitchen floor!"

"You're a nut!" Bess said, laughing and synchronizing her footsteps to match the tune.

Halfway up the block, they both collapsed against each other laughing.

"We haven't done that in years!" Bess said.

"Probably for a very good reason." Margaret reached into her purse to get a tissue—her cheeks were wet with tears. They had been laughing that hard. "We always had so much fun. Didn't we?"

Bess looked sad. "You make it sound as if we died."

The enormity of Bess's words struck Margaret in a part of her that she hadn't dared to explore.

"Maybe a part of us has," she said. "At least for a time."

Bess's eyebrows shot up. She started walking again—Margaret followed.

"I don't mean it the way it sounds," Margaret said. "It's just that suddenly things seemed to make sense. We're changing. That isn't bad, is it?"

"Is it?" Bess echoed. "I don't know. You're the one with all the mature answers."

It was a frightening sensation, having Bess sound so cold and remote. Margaret felt herself getting angry. Why didn't Bess understand? She wasn't trying to abandon her. Their lives were changing, that's all.

"I don't think you're being fair," Margaret said. "I just meant that maybe we both needed to accept some of the changes. I know this must be a very hard period for you—"

"Why is that?" Bess said. Her voice had a bitter edge to it.

Margaret wanted to say because it was the first time she was dating and Bess wasn't, but it seemed too cruel.

"Because of Lenny and stuff," Margaret said.

"'Stuff'? That doesn't seem to suit your new and profound understanding of the world. I must say, I'm very surprised."

Margaret stared at Bess, speechless. She didn't know what Bess expected of her.

"I need some time to think," Margaret said.

Bess turned to her. "Don't think so much. Feel it. Let it

all just sweep over you. Maybe then you'll be able to figure it all out."

With those final words, Bess turned and walked away.

Dumbfounded, Margaret watched as Bess became a dot in the distance. With a start, she realized that they had walked to the entrance of the park. This time, they hadn't been able to find comfort in the patterns of the past. Margaret hesitated for only a second—then she entered the park alone.

Chapter 10

Bess was in a rage. Nothing in her life was going right. She had made an absolute fool of herself with Margaret. At least fifty times she had picked up the phone to call Margaret—she just couldn't make herself dial the number. They avoided each other in school. It was really ridiculous. Several times Margaret had approached her, but Bess had coolly turned her back and looked the other way. She had really felt like throwing herself at Margaret's feet and begging her forgiveness, but she just couldn't. Stubborn. That's what was the matter with her. Stupid *and* stubborn. She had lost her boyfriend and her best friend—no small accomplishment for one person. She had seen Margaret and Zak together in the hallway at school a few times. They really looked cute together. Zak looked crazy about Margaret.

It was lonely walking home from school these days. Bess was so used to discussing the day's events with Margaret or Lenny. Now there was no one. It was really peculiar. Well, Sam would be home in a few weeks. Bess couldn't wait. He always managed to help her put things in perspective. It would be nice to sit up and talk all night with Sam. He always made her feel better.

Bess stopped along the way to look in the shop windows. She really needed some new clothes, but she just didn't feel like buying anything. Margaret had such good taste—a real flair for putting things together. She had a wonderful sense of color and texture. Her mother said Margaret had a lot of style. It was a word that suited her perfectly. Margaret always dragged Bess to the thrift shops on Second Avenue and in Greenwich Village to prowl among the rags. Margaret always managed to come up with something—a scarf, a blouse, a pair of lace gloves—something that was just the right addition for an outfit. She always looked so effortlessly put together. Bess always bought the same things—jeans and sweaters. Margaret told her that her taste was locked in. Bess just wasn't very good at change. She resisted it the way most people put off going to a dentist. There was always the hope that the toothache would disappear by itself. It was simply a matter of postponing the inevitable. Bess knew change was imminent—she had known it for some time. She just couldn't bear facing up to it. She was so busy trying to sort out all her thoughts, she hadn't even ralized that she had walked right past her house. Bess thought how typical it was of her to do that—she always walked right by the obvious. She was too damned analytical. Why couldn't she just go with the flow like everyone else? There were just too many things happening at once. Bess felt weary. She took the elevator to her floor and unlocked the door. Without bothering to remove her shoes, Bess flung her books across her desk and flopped down on her bed. Within seconds she was asleep.

The phone was ringing. Bess felt as if she were hearing the sound from the end of a long tunnel. She couldn't rouse herself from sleep. It had already grown dark outside, and the house was still. The illuminated dial on her clock radio said five-thirty. Had she really been asleep for that long? Where was her mother? The phone continued to ring with angry determination.

"Hello?" Bess's voice was hesitant and still heavy with sleep.

"Are you all right? What took so long to answer the phone?"

Her mother's concern shot through the darkness like a bolt of bright light—it warmed Bess.

"Mom? Where are you? I was sleeping."

Her mother's laugh sounded light and cheerful, as if *she* couldn't recognize that Bess had been sleeping.

"I suspected as much, dear," her mother said. "You don't sound exactly alert."

"Where are you?"

"I thought I'd surprise Daddy and pick him up from the office. We're going to have dinner out."

Her mother's voice was breathless and girlish. Bess was envious.

"That sounds nice, Mom."

"Are you sure you're all right? There's some cold chicken in the fridge. Please be sure to eat. Are you okay?"

"I'm fine. Really. Have a good time."

"Thanks, honey. I'll see you later. We won't be late."

Bess carefully hung up the phone. Margaret's number flashed across her eyes. But she turned over and went back to sleep.

She started planning her future. Maybe she would take up yoga and meditation and run away to a retreat. Tibet was supposed to be beautiful this time of the year. She scribbled in her notebook while Mr. Hathaway explained the consequences of the Industrial Revolution. Bess pretended to be fascinated by his explanation of child labor laws. She made a pretty good caricature of poor Mr. Hathaway—Margaret always said that they used his ears to pick up signals in outer space. Considering the size of his ears, it wasn't a totally unreasonable idea. Bess looked up from her doodling and noticed Pete Holten grinning at her. He was on the wrestling team with Lenny. In fact, he was a pretty good friend of

Lenny's. They had doubled more than a few times. Bess had recently heard that Pete and his girlfriend, Trish, had split up. Bess had never much liked Trish. She was always hanging on to Pete and giggling. Bess couldn't tolerate girls who giggled. Anyway, Pete was a really nice guy. Lenny thought he was the best wrestler on the team. He certainly had a great build. He was a lot more muscular than Lenny. Bess returned his smile and quickly looked away. He had a certain "energy" that she found both exciting and frightening. The look in his eyes told her he was aware of his effect on girls.

When the bell rang, Bess collected her books and purse and started walking out the door. Pete blocked her exit.

"Hi! I haven't seen much of you lately," Pete said.

"I've been here."

"In body, but not in spirit."

Bess laughed and tried to duck under his arm. He didn't budge.

"Hey, move!" she said. "There are other people eager to get into this class, and I'll be late for math."

"I'll walk you."

Bess eyed Pete suspiciously. He had quite a reputation around school. She didn't much feel like being added to his roster of girls.

"Why?" she said.

"I feel like it."

"Suit yourself." Bess shrugged and started walking.

Pete matched his stride to meet Bess's. He swung his books in one hand and with little effort. He was wearing cologne—Bess recognized a familiar musky smell, but she couldn't place it.

"Trish and I split up," Pete said.

"I heard."

"*I* heard about you and Lenny. Sorry."

"Sorry about you and Trish."

Pete grinned.

"Don't be," he said. "I'm not."

68

Bess decided not to say anything. Her mother always told her, if you have nothing nice to say, don't say anything at all. It had always seemed like pretty silly advice, but it was suitable for this set of circumstances.

"Are you dating?" Pete said.

"Dating?" The word caught in Bess's throat as if she had never heard of it before.

"Yeah, dating. You know, boy and girl go to movies and for a hamburger and whatever."

"Whatever?"

Pete laughed.

"I'm just teasing you," he said. "How about the first two?"

Bess bristled. She wondered if he was teasing her because Lenny had told him she was a prude or something. Guys were like that. They always talked about girls who did and didn't put out. Bess hated that expression. Sam used it all the time.

"Well?" Pete said. "What do you think?"

Bess eyed him carefully. He was really very handsome. She liked him, too. He was a lot different from Lenny. Pete was the kind of guy who was always slapping people on the back and making jokes. Lenny was so much more serious by comparison. She had never really understood their friendship. Well, it must be true that opposites attract.

"Okay," she said. "Why not?"

Pete smiled. "I don't know if I should be insulted or flattered."

"Does it matter?" She wondered if she'd start giggling soon—flirting was not her area of expertise.

"I guess not. Anyway, is Saturday all right?"

"Fine."

"I'll pick you up about six-thirty."

"Sounds great," Bess said. "I'll see you then."

She wondered why she had a sinking feeling in the pit of her stomach as she watched Pete walk away.

Bess decided not to think about Saturday. After all, it was just a date. It wasn't as if she didn't know Pete. They had been out together often enough. Still, when Saturday came, she emptied out her closet, looking for something to wear. The floor was piled with sweaters, and her bed was strewn with pants and skirts.

"I have nothing to wear!" Bess shouted. "I'll have to cancel my date."

Her mother cautiously knocked at the door.

"Come in," Bess said. "Enter at your own risk."

Her mother opened the door and stuck her head in.

"Isn't it a bit early for spring cleaning?" she said. "It could also be a bit late. What is going on in here?"

Bess plopped herself down on her bed amid her clothes and looked at her mother.

"I have nothing to wear! I have absolutely *nothing* to wear."

Her mother smiled. "I can see that," she said. "Your room looks positively bare."

"Oh, really! It's not funny. I have a date tonight, and I have nothing to wear."

Her mother raised an eyebrow and tried to mask her surprise. "A date?" she said. "With anyone I know?"

Bess pretended to be very busy looking over her sweaters. "In a sense," she said. "I don't know if you'd remember him."

"Try me." Her mother sat down on the edge of Bess's bed and studied Bess carefully.

"Pete Holten. You wouldn't remember him."

Her mother smiled and absently stroked one of Bess's stuffed animals. "Didn't Sammy give you this when you had your tonsils out?" she said. "Or was it the stuffed snake? I never seem to get those things straight."

"It was the snake. Do you remember him?"

"Certainly."

"Why didn't you say so?"

Her mother patted the space on the bed and beckoned Bess.

70

"Come sit with me for a few minutes," her mother said.

"What's the matter?" Bess said. "Don't you like Pete?"

"The question is, do you like him?"

Bess pulled at a thread on her jeans and looked quizzically at her mother.

"Sure, I like him. Why do you ask?"

"Don't get me wrong, Bessie. I'm glad you're going out. I know how difficult this period of your life must be. It's just that I don't want to see you get hurt."

"Can you prevent that?"

They sat a small distance apart—mother and daughter—time reflected in the space between them. Although strangers remarked on the striking physical resemblance between Bess and her father, the similarity at this moment between Bess and Ruth Ellis was startling. Something in the movements of their hearts made them the same. Bess sensed that her mother had known all her fears. Her mother smiled and patted Bess's hand.

"I wish I could," her mother said. "I remember when you would come crying to me over a pair of pants that had grown too short a week after we'd bought them. I guess I couldn't help you then, and I can't really help you now."

"Does that mean I'm a full-fledged adult?"

Her mother laughed and hugged Bess close to her. "Definitely not," she said. "It just means that I'm getting old!"

"You never answered my question."

"What question was that?"

"Do you like Pete?"

Her mother released her hold and took Bess's face in her hand. "I like him. He seems like a very nice boy. Very cute, too."

"Oh, really, Mom!"

Her mother started to pick over Bess's clothes. "Now what about this sweater?" She held up a beautiful black sweater with silver and red threads running through it. "I always loved this one on you."

Bess turned her face away. "Margaret bought me that for my birthday," she said. "I don't want to wear it."

Her mother seemed not to have heard. "She has such good taste. I'd completely forgotten that she bought it for you. Didn't she also get you a sash to wear with it? Wherever does that girl find these things?" She rummaged through Bess's dresser drawer, looking for the sash.

"I wish you wouldn't go through my things!" Bess snapped. "You know how much I hate it. I'll find something to wear on my own." Her voice was icy. Her mother looked startled—a pained expression crossed her face before she allowed anger to overtake her.

"That tone of voice is uncalled for. What's gotten into you? You're a regular Jekyll and Hyde. I can't figure you out at all."

Bess glared at her mother. "I would just like to have a little privacy," she said. "Is that so bad? I'm sick and tired of hearing about how wonderful Margaret is. I hear it at school, and I don't want to hear it at home!"

Her mother looked as if a light bulb had been flicked on over her head. She gently folded the black sweater and placed it on top of Bess's dresser. She gave it one last longing look.

"I take it you don't want to talk about whatever has happened between you and Margaret. Am I correct?"

"Absolutely," Bess said. "Anyway, nothing *happened*. We just seem to have outgrown each other. Doesn't that happen?"

"Sure it does. I just didn't see it coming with you and Margaret."

Bess took her terry cloth robe from the back of the door. "I have to take a shower. Pete will be here."

"I still think you should wear the sweater," her mother said. "It looks wonderful on you. And another thing—don't be as quick to throw away your friends as you are to discard your clothes."

She closed the door behind her and left Bess standing in the middle of the room with her cheeks burning.

"I said I didn't want to talk about it," Bess said to her mother's absent form. "Why doesn't anyone ever listen to me?"

Bess heard the doorbell ring just as she was tying the sash around her waist. She took one last look at herself in the mirror and picked up her hairbrush. She really needed a trim—she had been putting it off for weeks. She hated getting her hair cut—she always felt odd for at least a couple of weeks after.

She heard her mother's footsteps approaching. Neither of them had said a word to each other since their confrontation earlier this evening. Bess opened the door before her mother had a chance to knock.

"I'm ready," Bess said. "How do I look?"

She was wearing the sweater her mother had suggested. The sash was tied low on her hips and looked striking against the black velvet pants she had selected to complete the outfit.

"Beautiful," her mother said. "I like the sweater. Where did you get the pants?"

"Margaret made me buy them last season at Bloomingdale's—she said they were a steal. I've never worn them before."

"I'm glad you have reason to wear them now." She turned and started to walk away.

"Mom?"

Her mother stopped and looked over her shoulder at Bess.

"Yes?"

"About before . . ."

"You don't have to explain now. Peter is waiting."

"I want to. It's about Margaret. I just feel sort of funny talking about it. I don't really know what happened. That's why I got so upset."

Her mother turned back and entered Bess's room, closing the door behind them.

"The two of you have something very special. I'd hate to see you lose it because of something stupid."

"I know."

"Now get going. It's tacky to keep a date waiting."

Bess followed her mother into the living room. Pete was listening to her father tell one of his famous corny jokes. They both smiled when Bess and Ruth entered.

"Hi," Pete said. "Am I too early?"

"No. I'm always late."

Following a few pleasantries, Bess and Pete found themselves outside the door.

"Well," Pete said.

"Well," Bess said.

"I hate first dates."

Bess had not been prepared for such directness.

"Me, too."

"Why don't we pretend that it's our second date?"

"How about our third?"

They laughed comfortably. The first awful moment had passed. Bess relaxed and noticed that Pete had dimples. He was really very cute—her mother was right again.

"I thought we'd get a hamburger or something first," Pete said. "The movie doesn't start until nine-thirty."

"Sounds good."

They walked next to each other, leaving a safe distance between them. Pete was surpisingly quiet.

"What's on your mind?" Bess asked.

"I was just thinking that if this was our third date, I'd definitely be holding your hand."

Bess stopped for a moment and thought it over. He certainly had a very smooth style. Still, he *was* sweet and seemed sincere. She offered him her hand. He took it, and it didn't feel at all strange.

Chapter 11

Bess and Pete became inseparable almost immediately. It almost seemed as if there had never been a time in her life when Pete *hadn't* been around. She was struck by how unlike Lenny he was—not that she compared them. In fact, she often reminded herself how wonderful it was that she hardly thought of Lenny at all.

"What are you thinking about?" Pete said.

They were sitting in the school cafeteria, sharing a soggy hamburger. Pete took three bites to each of her one.

"What?" Bess said. She chewed slowly.

"What are you thinking about? You have a faraway look in your eyes."

Bess swallowed and smiled fondly. He *was* very handsome. All the girls in the school were crazy about him. His blond good looks and athletic build were not at all what usually attracted her, but she found herself excited by his enthusiasm and energy—not that she minded his well-developed biceps. She reached out and stroked his arm. He placed his hand over hers and squeezed.

"I was thinking about you," she said.

"I'm glad. I'd hate to think that look was for anyone else."

Pete released her hand and concentrated on his food. When he had finished his last french fry, he pushed the tray away.

"I'm still hungry. I'll get another burger. Do you want anything?"

Bess shook her head. "No. I'm fine."

"I'll be right back."

Bess watched him as he walked away. Other kids called out to him as he passed their tables. It seemed as if everyone in the school knew him. She noticed how many of the girls followed him with their eyes, sizing him up and smiling appreciatively. It gave her a warm feeling to know that he was hers.

"Taking stock of the merchandise?"

Bess looked up. "Lenny." It was all she could manage to say.

"I heard about you and Pete."

"News travels fast."

Lenny smiled and characteristically tugged at his ear—it was a habit Bess had found endearing. Now she felt irritated.

"Not *that* fast," Lenny said. "I just heard about it the other day. How long have you been seeing each other?"

"A couple of weeks."

"I'm surprised it took as long as it did."

Bess found that she didn't feel like talking to him. She wished Pete would hurry back.

"How's Ellen?" she said.

"The same. You seem different."

"Oh?"

He shifted uncomfortably from foot to foot.

"Do you mind if I sit down?"

Bess looked over her shoulder—Pete was nowhere in sight.

"I guess not," she said.

"Sure?"

Bess looked him full in the face for the first time since he had walked over—he looked tired.

"Sure," she said. She waited until he comfortably seated himself, stretching his legs out in front. "You look beat. Has Ellen been keeping you up?" She smiled coquettishly.

"You *have* changed. I remember when a remark like that would make you blush. Maybe all the locker room stories I've been hearing are true after all."

Bess tried not to show her surprise, but she felt her cheeks grow hot. She forced herself not to pursue the conversation—that was exactly what he wanted.

"I see you haven't forgotten how to blush," Lenny said. "I'm glad."

"What else are you glad about?" Bess said. "What do you want from me?"

Lenny gripped the edge of the table until his knuckles turned white. He leaned toward Bess until she could feel his breath on her face.

"How could you?" he said. "How could you go out with Pete? He's *my* friend—or rather, he *was* my friend. Now I've lost my best friend and my girlfriend."

"You still have Ellen." She was immediately sorry for her words. She knew how he felt.

Lenny looked startled, but he pulled himself together and smiled.

"You're right," he said. "I still have Ellen, and you still have Pete." He stood and looked down at her. "Just one more thing, Bess. Those stories I've been hearing? Your buddy, Pete, just laughs when the guys kid him. I thought you should know. Here he comes now. Why don't you ask him?"

Bess turned to look at Pete walking toward them. His smile quickly faded when he saw Lenny.

"I'll be seeing you," Lenny said. He turned and walked away before Pete reached them.

Bess felt her heart pounding. She didn't know what to think. How could she ask Pete if what Lenny had said was really true? What if it wasn't true? Worse, what if it really was true?

"What did *he* want?" Pete demanded.

"What took you so long?" Bess said. "I thought you just went to get a hamburger."

"I saw the coach. He wanted to talk to me. What did Lenny want?"

Bess decided it wasn't a good time to ask Pete if what Lenny had said was really true. She smiled. Pete's worried expression pleased her.

"Nothing much. Hurry up and eat your hamburger. It's almost time for class."

Pete didn't look convinced, but he obliged Bess. Between hurried mouthfuls, he pressed her for information.

"He was just being friendly. Honestly, Pete. I feel like I'm in some sort of absurd beach party movie. I wish you'd both leave me alone!"

The bell rang, and the entire cafeteria seemed to move at once.

"I've got to run," Bess said. "I have to get something from my locker. I'll see you after school."

She didn't bother to wait for Pete's answer—she didn't much feel like talking to anyone.

Bess raced up to the third floor with her head bent against the onslaught of bodies. She was going to be late again, and she didn't really feel like another confrontation with anyone. She sighed deeply as she pushed her way through the crowd.

"Is that what one could call a heartbreaking sigh?"

Bess turned to the side and saw Margaret trying to match her steps with her own. They hadn't spoken to each other since that awful day in front of the park. Bess couldn't think of anyone she would rather have bumped into.

"It's good to see you," Bess said.

"I believe that likewise is the appropriate response."

They smiled warmly at each other.

"This seems to be my day for reunions—but this is the best one," Bess said. "I've missed you. I should have called. I've been a real—"

"Forget it," Margaret said. "I didn't exactly do anything to help matters."

The late bell rang. The halls were suddenly silent.

"Damn it!" Bess said. "I'm late again. When can we talk?"

"After school?"

Bess hesitated. "I sort of had plans."

Margaret smiled. "Pete?"

"How did you know?"

"Doesn't everyone?"

Bess tried to take it as it was meant—an innocent remark. Still, she couldn't help feeling more than slightly uncomfortable.

"I'll explain to Pete," Bess said. "I'll meet you in front of my locker."

"I'll see you later."

"Later," Bess said. She felt better already. It felt as if she hadn't spoken to Margaret in years, instead of only two weeks. Now all she had to worry about was explaining to Pete.

"I thought the two of you weren't speaking," Pete said. His voice had a hard, suspicious edge to it that Bess found disturbing.

"You sound disappointed that we decided to make up," Bess said. "I don't understand you."

Bess was rummaging through her locker, trying to locate her history book. Between her stuff and Pete's sneakers and books, it was an impossible task.

"Why do you have to shove everything in my locker?" she said. "I can't find a damned thing. I don't see what you're so upset about. I'll speak to you later. We've been together every day for almost two weeks. I need some female companionship." She slammed the locker door with a resolute bang.

Pete bent over and turned her face toward his. "That's not the message you've been sending me," he said. He started to kiss her along the neck.

"What are you doing?" Bess said, shoving him away. "Don't do that in school. You know how I feel about that stuff."

"I thought I did. You certainly don't seem to mind it when we're on your couch."

Bess was so startled that for a moment she couldn't catch her breath. She stared at him, unable to think of a word to say.

"Why do you look so stunned?" he said. "It's true, isn't it?"

Bess had a sudden urge to slap him across the face, but it just seemed too dramatic—appropriate, but too dramatic.

"I've got to go," she said. "Margaret'll be waiting."

"What's with you, anyway? You're hot and cold. One minute you're looking at me with adoration, and the next minute you're running off to meet your stupid girlfriend. I thought we were going to go to your house and, you know, be together."

"Be together? You mean fool around, don't you, Pete? That's all you want to do."

"Is that bad? I like you. I enjoy fooling around with you. I thought you enjoyed it as much as I do."

"Is that what you tell all the guys?"

It was Pete's turn to be speechless. He recovered quickly, and a nasty look crossed his face. "Is that what loverboy told you?" he said. "Good ol' Lenny. Mr. Honesty strikes again."

"Look, Pete. I don't want to get into this with you right now. Maybe it's a good idea for us to have a break for a few days. We've been spending a lot of time together."

"No!"

She was caught off guard by his anger. She took a step back, as if he had made a move to strike her.

"You started this," he said. "Now, you finish it!"

The few people in the hallway started to gather.

"You're making a scene," Bess said. "Can't we talk about this when we're both a little calmer?"

She saw Margaret turning the corner—she never stopped to rubberneck. She was deep in conversation with Zak.

"Margaret!" Bess said. She turned back to Pete, who was still glaring at her. "Please, Pete. I just don't feel up to fighting with you."

Before he had a chance to answer, Margaret and Zak were standing next to them.

"Hi," Margaret said. "Pete, do you know Zak? Well, now you do. Pete meet Zak. Zak meet Pete."

They shook hands and nodded.

"Are we interrupting something?" Margaret said. She turned to Bess. "Should I wait for you outside?"

"No," Bess said. "I'm ready."

"Are you walking out with us?" Margaret said, turning to Pete.

"I don't think so," Pete said. "Don't you know that old saying, three's company, four's a crowd? Catch you all later."

Without even looking at Bess, he turned and walked away. Bess watched his retreating form and shrugged helplessly.

"There goes a happy man," Margaret said. "Wouldn't you agree?"

"Shut up," Zak said. "Your cheery good humor isn't making things any better."

Bess was surprised at how easily Margaret accepted Zak's command. She faced them and offered a halfhearted smile.

"I seem to be batting a thousand today," she said.

"That's an understatement," Zak said.

Bess laughed and nodded to show her agreement.

"Zak's very perceptive," Margaret said. "He has a truly extraordinary mind."

"*Merci,*" Zak said. "Now, ladies, shall I leave you to your devices, or shall I escort you from the building as we engage in idle small talk?"

"Get lost," Margaret said. She gave him a playful shove. "I'll speak to you later."

Zak kissed her chastely on the cheek and turned, clicking his heels, to face Bess. He reached for her hand and held it in his. "My dear woman," he said. "It has been both an honor and a pleasure to know you. I trust you will have a pleasant afternoon. Ladies, I take leave of you."

"Just take leave, would ya?" Margaret said.

Zak smiled sweetly. "Ah, my little dove. Your command of the language thrills me. Until later." He bowed ceremoniously and walked away.

"He's adorable," Bess said. "I like him."

"So do I. What happened? I have a feeling we walked in on World War III."

"Can we talk about it later? We have all afternoon. Where do you want to go?"

"Anyone home at your house? Janie and my mom are home at mine."

"My house is empty. Let's go."

Bess was grateful that Margaret didn't push her for details as they walked toward the bus stop. The air was chill and raw—Thanksgiving was next week. She wondered if Margaret was still interested in Sam. She seemed so absorbed with Zak, and deservedly so—he was bright and funny and clearly crazy about her. The bus was on the corner, and they ran to catch it.

"God!" Margaret said. She slumped into her seat. "I'm exhausted. We've been rehearsing every night."

"I'm glad you got the part," Bess said. "You deserve it."

"*I* think so. Anyway, it's been a lot of work. Mr. Rand is a total perfectionist. Talk about dedication—that guy knows Shakespeare inside and out."

"You look great. Have you lost more weight?"

"A grand total of fifteen pounds. What do you think?"

"Sensational," Bess said. "You seem really happy."

"Happy," Margaret said. "I don't know about *really* happy. That seems an awful lot to ask for. Don't you think?"

"Oh, I don't know what I think about anything anymore. Honestly, Meg, I've always had everything so together. Lately, no matter what I do, everything turns out wrong."

"The bigger they are, the harder they fall."

Bess gave Margaret a look that said it all. "I'd forgotten how tactless you could be," Bess said. "How does Zak stand you?"

"He's crazy about me. Just like you are."

Bess laughed. "I'm really sorry about what happened that day."

"I told you to forget about it."

"I don't want to forget about it," Bess said. "I want to talk about it. I guess I'm scared."

"Scared? Of what?"

"Everything is changing. First this whole thing with Lenny. Then you. Now Pete. I can't figure out what's going on."

"I believe it's called life," Margaret said. "I've heard rumors that it changes all the time."

"Why?" Bess said. "Why does it have to change so quickly? I can't keep up."

"It doesn't change so quickly. It's just that it changes all at once—it's an illusion. It just sort of sneaks up on you. It can be hell, *if* you're not prepared. And you, my dear friend, were obviously not prepared."

"You're beginning to sound just like Zak."

"I know. Doesn't it give you a chill?"

They laughed. Margaret turned to look out the window. She reached up to pull the signal cord. "C'mon," she said. "We almost missed our stop."

The bus lurched to a halt, and they scrambled down the steps.

"I feel as if I haven't been to your house in ages," Margaret said. "I'm starving. What did you have for dinner last night?"

"Chicken. I'll make us some sandwiches."

"Sounds good."

They rode the elevator in comfortable silence. Bess fumbled in her purse for the keys and withdrew them triumphantly in less than three minutes.

"Houdini would be proud," Margaret said. "I know I'm very impressed."

Bess unlocked the door and threw her books on the dining room table.

"I just want to change," she said. "Help yourself."

Minutes later, Bess returned to find Margaret munching on an apple.

"Whole wheat or rye?" Bess said. She pulled a foil-wrapped plate from the refrigerator.

"If there's any white meat left, I'll just take a piece," Margaret said. "I don't know why I'm so hungry. Curiosity does that to me every time."

Bess continued pulling away at the chicken carcass, seeming to ignore Margaret's words.

"And to think," Bess said, "I was congratulating myself on having a friend who doesn't believe in prying. You never know people, do you?"

Margaret stood and threw her apple core into the garbage. She walked over to Bess and draped an arm across her shoulder.

"Which friend was that?" she said.

"Certainly not you!"

"I'm sorry, but I'm dying to know. Pete Holten. Of all the unlikely people for you to date . . ." Margaret let her words trail off after Bess gave her an exasperated look. "Sorry. I didn't mean anything. It was just so sudden."

"Didn't you just tell me that life is like that?"

"Yes, but—"

"But, nothing," Bess said. "I always liked Pete. I'll agree, he's not exactly my type, but he's very sweet."

"What do you talk about? Wrestling? Football?"

"Don't be such a snob. Not everyone has to be an intellectual giant. Anyway, we just started dating. Right after you and I had a fight—"

"Don't tell me that I drove you to Pete Holten?"

Bess slammed the plates down on the table. "Here," she said. "Eat something. That way I won't have to listen to you."

Margaret sat down at the table. "I'm glad we're getting along so well."

Bess brought a loaf of bread, a jar of mayonnaise, and some sliced tomato to the table. She started to make herself a sandwich, thickly spreading the mayonnaise on two slices of bread. She licked the knife before putting it down.

"It would be nicer," Bess said, "if you'd give me a chance to finish a sentence."

"I'm sorry."

Bess carefully arranged chicken and slices of tomato between the bread. She pressed down on the sandwich to flatten it. She looked pleased with the results. "I need some pickles," she said.

Margaret grabbed her arm before she could get up. "Forget the pickles," she said. "Start talking."

"He excites me," Bess said. She took a big bite of her sandwich.

Margaret studied her carefully. "Go on," she said.

"That's it."

"What do you mean, 'that's it'?"

"Exactly what I said. He's nice. Well, at least he was up until today. We don't have very deep conversations. We talk, but not about anything really important. I like being with him. He's fun, and he excites me."

"Now, let's get down to the nitty-gritty. Have you slept with him?"

Bess got up from the table and went to the refrigerator. "Want some juice?"

"No, thanks. Well, maybe. What kind?"

"Orange or grapefruit. Wait, there's some apple, too."

"Apple. Well, have you?"

Bess poured the juice slowly. She shook her head without looking at Margaret. "No, it hasn't even come up yet."

"My goodness," Margaret said. "And to think it hasn't even been two weeks."

"Why do you have to be so sarcastic?" Bess said. "I'm trying to be honest with you, and you keep acting like a jerk."

"You're right. I'm sorry. I'm just having a hard time believing what I'm hearing. My next question is, do you want to sleep with him?"

Bess sat down at the table and handed Margaret a glass. "I don't know what I want. I do and I don't."

"Which part does and which part doesn't?"

"That should be pretty obvious. My body does, but my head doesn't."

"Go with your head," Margaret said. "Never trust your body."

"Lenny never really made me feel this way," Bess said. "There was so much feeling with him. So much emotion, but it was different physically."

"I think it's called lust."

"How do you know?"

"I read a lot," Margaret said. "Listen to me. Never trust your hormones. They'll do you in every time."

"How do your hormones feel about Zak?"

"As far as Zak is concerned, my hormones are quite safe. He's a very special guy, and I really like him. Still, my heart doesn't lurch when he's around."

"It's too bad," she said, "that we can't find a guy to match up with your feelings for Zak and my hormones for Pete. You know what I mean?"

Margaret smiled, but she didn't agree or disagree. Bess took another bite of her sandwich and decided not to mention that Sam would be home next week—she had a feeling that Margaret knew.

Chapter 12

Margaret left Bess's house just as the sky was turning dark—it was still early, but winter was approaching. Just as Bess closed the door after her, the phone rang.

She caught it on the second ring. No one there. She hung up immediately. There were too many weird people around to take chances. She tried not to think about who the caller might have been. Instead, she read the note her mother had left for her on the refrigerator. "Bess, darling—Will be home by seven. Please peel the potatoes and put them up to boil. Chicken again tonight. Put the tray in the oven at 350°. A salad would be wonderful. Love you. Mom."

Bess turned on the radio and flicked the dial until she found her favorite station—soft rock. She didn't go for any of the new punk stuff, and she couldn't stand disco. She hummed softly to herself as she took the potatoes from the plastic vegetable bin at the side of the sink. Her mother refused to use a potato peeler. "A good paring knife is much faster," Ruth always said. Still, they had at least half a dozen peelers in the utensil drawer. Bess smiled as she thought about her mother's stubbornness—she had inherited it, along with her quick temper. Sam was much more like their father—laid-back and easy to please. It was funny how different a brother and sister could be. Still, Bess was looking forward to seeing Sam—they had a lot to talk about.

The doorbell rang just as Bess finished peeling the last potato. It was still early—perhaps it was her mother. She dried her hands on a dish towel and called out, "Coming!" The bell continued to ring persistently. "Mom?" she said, but there was no answer. Remembering to look through the peephole, she caught a glimpse of a blond head—it was Pete.

"Bess," he said. "Open up. It's just me. I'm unarmed."

Cautiously she unlatched the door and opened it halfway.

"Hi," she said.

"Hi. Can I come in?"

He seemed to have calmed down from the afternoon, and she was relieved.

"I'm surprised to see you," she said. "I would have called."

Pete followed her into the kitchen.

"I'm getting dinner started," she said. "My parents will be home soon."

She wondered why she felt the need to caution him about her parents' impending arrival. Could it be that she didn't trust him? She pushed the thought from her mind and turned to Pete, who had already comfortably seated himself at the kitchen table.

"Are you hungry?" she said.

"Some milk would be great."

She took the container from the refrigerator and brought it to the table together with a large glass.

"No cookies?" she said.

Pete shook his head.

Bess filled the glass to the brim. As she turned to put the milk away, Pete caught her arm and pulled her toward him. She automatically tensed and gently released herself from his hold. Neither of them acknowledged the action until Bess spoke.

88

"I'm sorry," she said. "I'm a little edgy."

Pete took a gulp of milk. "I can see that," he said. "Any special reason?"

Bess tried to avoid looking at him—she was surprised that he was so unaware that her tension resulted from his presence. Could he really be so insensitive? Lenny had been able to read all of her responses with uncanny accuracy. She knew it wasn't a fair comparison—after all, she and Pete had only been dating for two weeks. How could you compare that to more than a year of shared time? Still, Lenny had been tuned in to her from the onset. She suddenly realized that Pete was regarding her with curiosity as she allowed her thoughts to wander.

"I have to make a salad," she said. It sounded even stupider after she heard her own words. What was wrong with her anyway?

Pete seemed determined to remain undaunted by her strange behavior.

"I was wondering when you would make the salad," he said. "I didn't dare to ask—the suspense was too much."

Bess laughed to cover her embarrassment.

Pete stood and walked over to where Bess was standing. He gently touched her elbow and turned her around. She faced him and smiled. For the first time, she noticed a birthmark on the right side of his neck and wondered why she had never seen it before. She tilted her face up to meet his kiss and allowed her body to be drawn against his. She tried not to think about anything as she felt his lips graze her neck and gently tug at her earlobe. His mouth found hers again, and she returned his kisses with equal enthusiasm. He was a wonderful kisser—so much more inventive and self-assured than Lenny had *ever* been. She was angry at herself for thinking about Lenny even while Pete was kissing her.

"Now," Pete murmured into her ear, "isn't this better than fighting?"

Bess thought it was a depressingly characteristic thing to

say, even though it might be true. She tried not to dwell on his comment—she had to concentrate on his hands as they traveled along the outline of her body. She wasn't sure that giving him access was the smartest thing to do.

"My parents will be home soon," she said. "I have to finish making the salad." She covered his hands with her own but didn't pull them away.

"You already told me," he said. He continued to move his hands about in spite of the pressure of her hands over his own.

She began to feel uncomfortable about his presence.

"I think we should stop now," she said. "Really."

Pete had started to unbutton her blouse, and she felt panic grip her.

"C'mon," he said. "They won't be here for at least an hour. I read the note."

He had already managed to undo the top three buttons with one hand—his other hand pressed her firmly against him.

"They're usually early," she said. Her blouse was now completely open—she was grateful that she was wearing a bra. "Really, Pete. I think we should stop."

Pete reached down a hand and swiftly undid the snap on her jeans. The noise seemed to echo in the large kitchen as if a cannon had been fired—it spurred Bess into action.

"What the hell do you think you're doing?" she said. She pulled away from his hold and quickly snapped her jeans, while holding her blouse closed. "Are you nuts?"

"Apparently," he said. He had folded his arms across his chest and was watching Bess as she tried to pull herself together. She had turned her back to him as she buttoned her blouse.

"Really," she said. "I can't figure you out."

"My thoughts exactly."

"What's that supposed to mean?" She turned to face him and smoothed her hair.

"C'mon, Bess," he said. "Grow up. You know you

wanted me to. You can't tell me that you and Lenny *never* did it. I mean, really, you were going together for at least a year. I just figured that it was a question of time until you'd do it with me. You can't tell me that you didn't want to. Besides, if you really loved me . . .."

Bess felt as if she were a shock victim. She knew that she was standing in the kitchen with Pete, but his face seemed to be floating somewhere above her. She couldn't quite make out his features. She felt his voice was disembodied. Her own flesh felt moist and clammy. She tried to speak, but her voice caught in her throat. Finally, she shook herself as if waking from a deep sleep.

"I'd like you to leave," she said. "I'd like you to leave—now." Her words were barely audible. The steady hum of the refrigerator motor was louder than her own voice. Pete gave her a blank stare.

"I want you to leave," she repeated. She felt the tears burning behind her eyes. She didn't want to cry in front of him. "Please, Pete."

He looked at her and smiled. "I guess I had you figured all wrong. I thought we had something going. Something good. You know what I mean?"

Bess couldn't believe he didn't understand the enormity of what had taken place. He was indignant over *her* behavior! She couldn't believe it. She had a sudden urge to laugh at the absurdity of it all. She felt slightly hysterical and tried to take a few deep breaths in order to steady herself. She inhaled slowly and concentrated on the rhythm of her body. She felt the tension leave her arms and neck. She was beginning to come back to life. Pete was still talking.

". . . and here I thought that we were really going places. I mean, there are lots of girls in school who would give anything to go out with me. I really like you, Bess. I mean, I *really* like you. I don't know why you couldn't just let nature take its course."

Bess looked at him and couldn't understand how she had

been so wrong. She had known about his reputation, but people talked. She had always tried not to listen to rumors. In a way, she was relieved. At least, it was over.

"I guess I just didn't *love* you enough," she said. Even Pete could not miss the sarcasm in her tone. She had taken aim and fired a direct hit. "Now, I'd like you to leave."

Pete tried to recover by looking at her and shaking his head. "Your loss, sweetheart," he said. "Believe me, you'll regret it."

Bess wordlessly followed him to the door.

"See ya around," he said.

Bess slammed the door shut and wondered how many years it would be before she could think of this day without feeling like an absolute fool.

"Bessie? Are you sick?"

Her mother's voice was soft and concerned. She placed a cool hand aganist Bess's forehead. "You don't seem to have a fever. What is it, honey? Are you all right?"

Bess struggled to open her eyes. She wondered what time it was. Had the chicken burned? She had put the tray in the oven and decided to rest for a few minutes.

"What time is it?" Bess said. Her voice sounded thick with sleep. She was incredibly thirsty.

"Seven-fifteen," her mother said. "Daddy and I just got home."

"Did the chicken burn?"

"Hardly," her mother said. "You forgot to turn the oven on."

Bess bolted upright. "I'm sorry," she said. "I can't believe it's only seven-fifteen. I couldn't have been sleeping for more than a half an hour."

Her mother pushed her back against the pillows. "It's okay," she said. "We'll have it tomorrow. Daddy went to get some pizza. Is that all right?"

"Fine. Fine."

"Are you sure you're all right?"

Bess sat up and touched her mother's hand reassuringly. "I'm fine. Just tired."

Her mother stood and smiled down knowingly at Bess.

"I have a feeling you're not telling me everything, but I'll have to settle for the fact that you're not sick. I'm going to go change. Why don't you throw some cold water on your face? I'll meet you inside."

Bess hugged her knees as she watched her mother's retreating form. She was glad she hadn't pressed her. She really didn't feel like talking. She decided to take her mother's advice. She stumbled into the bathroom and spashed her face with cold water. Now she had to worry about facing Pete in school. Life certainly wasn't getting any easier.

Her father was already back with the pizza when Bess walked into the kitchen.

"Hi, Daddy," she said. She planted a kiss on top of his balding head.

"Hello, stranger," Carl said. "I feel as if I haven't seen you in ages."

Ruth was getting paper plates from the cupboard. She took jars of oregano and hot red pepper from the spice rack and brought everything to the table.

"What are you drinking?" she said.

"Beer," Carl said.

"Is it cold enough?"

"Absolutely. What about you, Bess?"

Bess had placed both hands on top of the pizza box—the heat felt good. She couldn't help feeling chilled inside. Her parents exchanged a concerned look that she caught out of the side of her eye.

"Does hot chocolate sound too gross?" she said. "With pizza, I mean."

She could tell that her mother knew she had seen her. Her tone was too bright when she answered.

"Hot chocolate sounds divine," Ruth said. "I'll have some myself."

"I'll make it," Bess said.

Her father read the paper, innocent of the conspiratorial smiles exchanged between Bess and Ruth.

"Crime is getting worse and worse," he said. "Where is it all going to end?"

Bess stood by the stove, waiting for the water to boil.

Her mother winked at her. Carl was prone to lengthy tirades on troublesome social issues. Crime was one of his favorites.

"I mean, what's a family man to do?" he said. "I refuse to run away from the city. I was born and raised here. No one is going to make me leave my home."

Bess poured the boiling water into two waiting mugs. She had heard her father's speech a million times. She could practically recite it herself.

"Sam says it's better in Boston," she said. "He told me people walk around there at all hours of the night. Students, that is."

"Of course, but that's different. You'll find the same thing in any area where the college is the center of the community. There's still plenty of crime in Boston."

"Let's eat," Ruth said. "I'm starving."

Bess brought the steaming mugs to the table and took a seat between her parents. She pulled a slice of pizza apart from the rest of the pie. She was hungrier than she'd thought. She listened to her parents discuss Thanksgiving dinner plans as she munched on a big bite of pizza.

"I thought it would be nice to have just the four of us this year," Ruth said. "I'm tired of huge family gatherings. Besides, we won't be seeing Sam again until the Christmas break. What do you think, Bess?"

Bess enjoyed the whole family's getting together. She didn't often get a chance to see all her aunts, uncles, and cousins who lived out of town. Her father was the only one who stubbornly refused to leave the city. Bess was glad. She didn't think she would like living in a small town.

"Whatever you think," Bess said. "It doesn't really matter."

"I like the idea of the four of us," Carl said. "Maybe we'll go see the parade first. The more I think about it, the more I like it!"

Bess felt vaguely depressed. Why hadn't she spoken up? Her mother had wanted her opinion. She could have said that she liked getting together with the whole family on Thanksgiving. Her Aunt Rose made the best pumpkin pie, and she hadn't seen Sally in almost a year. They were the same age and had been best friends until the family moved to someplace upstate. Bess picked the cheese off her slice and discarded the crust.

"What's the matter?" Ruth said. "You look upset."

"I'm just tired. I told you before." Her tone was harsher than she had intended for it to be.

"Maybe you'd like to invite Pete," Carl said. "I like that boy. He's really going places. I can tell. He has a way about him."

"You can say that," Bess said. "No, thanks. I'm sure he has plans." She rose and put her mug in the sink.

"I think I'll say good night," she said. "I have some homework to do."

Without waiting for her parents to answer, she walked out of the kitchen and went to her room. Closing the door behind her, she threw herself across her bed and tried to sort out her feelings. She had let Pete get away with murder, and she had treated her parents badly. It just didn't seem to make sense. She would have to apologize to her parents tomorrow. Her father had also fallen for Pete's charms. Maybe she wasn't such a jerk, after all. Her dad had always been a pretty good judge of character. Everyone made mistakes. Pete was a whole other story. She should have said something to him. She had allowed him to walk all over her. The more she thought about it, the angrier it made her. She wouldn't have any peace until she settled this thing with him. She wasn't going to let him get away with it! Reaching for the phone, she recited his number aloud. Without hesitating, she dialed. He answered on the first ring.

"Hello?" Pete said.

"Pete. It's Bess. I have something to say to you."

"I hope it's good."

Bess decided to ignore his comment and simply say what she had briefly rehearsed in her head. "You were right," she said.

Even Pete seemed startled by that. "I was?"

"Remember you said I'd regret it? Well, I do."

"You do?"

Bess paused to take a deep breath. "I do. I regret ever having gone out with you in the first place!"

She slammed down the phone before he had a chance to answer.

Her parents were still in the kitchen when she walked in. Her mother was wrapping the leftover pizza in aluminum foil while her father read aloud from the paper. They both looked up when she entered.

"Sorry about before," Bess said. "It must have been the pizza. Anyway, I just wanted to say that the four of us sounds really nice for Thanksgiving. Maybe we could see the family soon, though. It's been a while, and I miss them." She smiled brightly at her parents' startled looks. "Well, good night."

She kissed them both and left them with their mouths formed in identical little *o*'s.

She brushed her teeth and washed her face. She climbed into bed and snuggled down between her sheets. Just before she drifted off to sleep, she thought, *You knocked off two guys in one month. Not bad, Bess. Not bad at all.*

She slept deeply and peacefully, looking forward to morning with anticipation—she had an awful lot to tell Margaret. An awful lot.

Chapter 13

Bess considered it a small miracle that she hadn't run into either Lenny or Pete at school. She had seen Ellen Duncan in the washroom, but Ellen was so busy admiring herself in the mirror that she had never even noticed.

"I still think you should have worn a disguise," Zak said.

Both Bess and Margaret shoved him at the same time. They were all walking home from school. They were looking forward to the long Thanksgiving weekend. Zak was leaving that afternoon for his grandmother's in Pennsylvania. Margaret was going to her aunt and uncle's in New Jersey. Bess was suddenly excited about the quiet family dinner her mother had been preparing for all week.

"What time are you leaving?" Margaret said, turning to look at Zak.

"I don't really know. Whenever my folks get home," he said. "I'm really going to miss you. Will you write?"

Zak put his arm around her and pulled her against his shoulder. Margaret rested her head there briefly and laughed. She looked at Bess and smiled.

"He's nuts. Don't you think so?"

"Nuts, but cute," Bess said.

"Thank you, madam," Zak said. He bowed deeply.

"You may borrow my Groucho Marx glasses and nose anytime you need to travel incognito."

"You're too kind," Bess said.

They reached the crosswalk and waited for the light to change. Bess watched Zak slip a protective arm around Margaret's waist. They looked good together. She had wondered how Margaret felt about Sam coming home. So far, neither one of them had mentioned him other than to acknowledge that he would be in that evening.

"C'mon," Zak said. "You look as if you're in another world." He held out a hand to her as they started to cross the street. Bess reached for his hand and smiled. He really was a very nice guy. Margaret was lucky.

"Well," Zak said. "I guess this is where we part."

They all stood on the corner huddled together against the wind.

"Should I leave you two alone?" Bess said. "I hate mushy good-byes."

"Don't worry," Margaret said. "We're very formal." She held out her hand to Zak. "See?"

Bess laughed and averted her eyes as Zak pulled Margaret toward him and kissed her. It didn't take more than a few seconds, but she felt uncomfortable. She wasn't used to being the one standing on the side. Now she knew how Margaret must have felt all those times it had been the two of them and Lenny.

"Have a good weekend," Zak said. He reached over and kissed Bess lightly on the cheek. "Your brother is coming in today, right?"

Bess nodded. She avoided looking at Margaret. There was an awkward silence.

"Well," he said. "I'd better get going. I have a list a mile long of a 'few things' my grandmother needs. I'll be seeing you."

"Have a good time," Margaret said. She kissed him again and patted his cheek. "Call me on Sunday."

He winked and turned to walk away. Bess and Margaret

stood silently, watching his retreating form. He turned once to wave. Margaret raised her hand and waved back. Bess huddled down inside her jacket.

"It's getting cold," she said. "Are you ready?"

"Hmm? Oh, sure. Sorry. I was just thinking."

They started walking. The streets were crowded with people hurrying home. Most everyone was out of work earlier than usual.

"He's really nice," Bess said. "I like him a lot."

Margaret didn't answer.

"I think he's in love with you," Bess said. "You should see the way his face lights up when he looks at you."

Margaret still didn't say anything. Bess wondered if she had heard her.

"Margaret?"

"I heard you. I don't know what to say."

"I don't understand."

Margaret stopped walking and turned to look directly at her. Bess saw that Margaret's face was flushed, and her eyes bright. She really looked beautiful. She had cut her hair in a new style—it was layered and angled in toward her face. It made her look a lot older and more sophisticated.

"He *is* in love with me," Margaret said. "The thing is, I'm not in love with him."

It was Bess's turn to be quiet. She was pretty sure she knew what was coming.

"I really care about him," Margaret continued. "You know I do. He's sweet, and smart, and funny. I've even gotten used to his strange way of talking. He's absolutely wonderful to me."

"So?" Bess said.

Margaret looked deeply into Bess's eyes for a lingering moment and then looked quickly away.

"Let's walk," she said. "It's getting too cold."

"We can walk, but the question stands."

Margaret stopped again and grabbed Bess's arm.

"Every time he kisses me, I can't help wondering what it would be like to kiss Sam."

She had blurted out the whole sentence without taking one breath. They were silent. Bess tried to think of something to break the tension.

"It's no big deal," she said. "It doesn't do a thing for me."

They looked at each other and laughed. Passersby stopped to stare at them. They were hysterical, holding their stomachs and doubled over.

"It wasn't that funny," Bess said. She was gasping for breath.

"I know. *That's* what's so funny."

They pulled themselves together and started walking again.

"I don't know what to tell you," Bess said. "I can't give Sam to you."

"I know that."

"When will you be back from Jersey?"

"Friday morning."

"Why don't you come over?"

Margaret smiled. "I thought you'd never ask."

"Maybe everything will work out," Bess said.

"I'm sure it will," Margaret said. "I'll make it work out."

They reached the corner at which they normally separated.

"Are you all right?" Margaret said. "I mean about Pete and all?"

"Perfect. Honest."

They waved good-bye and smiled. Bess watched Margaret as she turned the corner and wondered if Sam would even recognize her.

The apartment was dark when Bess opened the door, but she had an eerie feeling that someone was there beside her.

"Mom? Dad? Is anyone home?"

She turned the hall light on and put her books on the

dining room table. She was sure she heard something from one of the back rooms.

"Mom? Dad?"

"How about 'Sam'?"

Bess jumped and gasped as she turned to face Sam.

"You scared the life outta me! When did you get home? I thought you were coming in tonight."

He was drying his hair with a towel. He was bare-chested, and Bess couldn't help notice how handsome he was.

"Does that mean you're not glad to see me?" he said.

She stood on her tiptoes and kissed his cheek.

"I'm very glad to see you. Did you call Mom?"

"This morning. You had left already. I caught a ride down with one of the guys."

"Are you hungry?"

"I ate. I see Mom stocked up."

"For you, anything."

"Cut it out. C'mon, help me unpack."

She followed him to his room. The furniture gleamed. Everything was in perfect order except for his suitcase and clothes strewn all over the bed.

"You're upsetting the shrine," Bess said. "Mom's been cleaning for a week."

She squeezed in alongside his clothes and bags. She found a comfortable position and rested her head on one hand. She watched Sam as he opened his suitcase and pulled out a sweatshirt.

"I brought you this," he said. He held out the sweatshirt.

Bess sat up and took the Boston University sweatshirt. She placed it against her chest and looked down.

"Thanks, but couldn't you have brought a bigger chest with it?"

Sam laughed. "I thought you knew that small boobs were very fashionable."

"In what tribe?"

"Somewhere in New Guinea, I think."

"I'll move."

Sam sat down on the bed next to her. He put his hands behind his head and leaned back, stretching out his legs.

"So," he said, "bring me up to date."

"On what?"

"What's the boyfriend situation these days?"

"That won't take long—there is no situation."

"What happened to Pete?"

"Nothing happened to Pete. I just decided he wasn't right for me."

"How come?"

Bess pulled a loose thread on the bedspread. She didn't really feel like answering a million questions. She didn't think he would understand anyway.

"Oh, a million reasons. You know how it is," she said.

"I'm not sure I do."

Bess got off the bed and went to stand near the window. She remembered how she used to watch all the people and make up stories about them. It seemed to be a very long time ago. Sam had taught her to roller-skate down this hill, warning her that one wrong move would definitely result in a broken head. How old had she been? Eight or nine? She couldn't remember.

"How old was I when you taught me to skate down this hill?" She kept her back to him. "Do you remember?"

Sam laughed. "Remember? I couldn't forget a thing like that. You got the skates for your eighth birthday. You wanted everyone to go home so you could try them out. Mom got really mad at you."

It was Bess's turn to laugh. "God, was I stubborn." She turned to smile at him. "Wasn't I?"

"I'm not sure 'wasn't' is exactly the right word. How about are?"

Bess sat down on the bed again and leaned against his bags.

"I thought we were going to unpack," she said. "Should

I start with this one?" She pointed at his garment bag. "What did you bring in this?"

"A sports jacket and stuff."

"How come?"

"I have a very heavy date. Leave everything. I'll do it. Just keep me company." He got up and started pulling things from the suitcase. Most everything looked wrinkled and dirty. "I didn't have a chance to do laundry this week."

"Who's the girl?" Bess started sorting his laundry into two piles—dark and light. She tried not to seem too interested.

"A girl from school. She's an art history major. She's also very gorgeous."

"Is she from New York?"

Sam went to his closet and looked for a wooden hanger. "No. She's visiting some relatives. She's from Vermont. We went skiing together last year with a whole bunch of people. I just got up enough nerve to ask her out."

Bess walked over to the closet and immediately found a wooden hanger. She handed it to Sam. "That doesn't sound like you."

"You'd have to see Kate to understand. She's really something."

"It sounds serious."

Sam took a pair of tan slacks from the garment bag and inspected them. "Do you think I could get these for Saturday if I took them to the cleaner today?"

"I think so. Tell him it's an emergency. It always makes him feel important. Is it?"

"An emergency?"

"No. Is it serious?"

He looked at her and squinted his eyes. "Why do I feel as if I'm getting the third degree?"

"Maybe because you are."

"Any special reason?"

"Sisterly curiosity."

"I don't buy it. Anyway, you haven't given me any information about Lenny or Pete."

She rolled her eyes and folded her hands across her chest. "All right. What do you want to know?"

"Well for one thing, do you think you did the right thing in not sleeping with Lenny?"

"That remains to be seen. Next question."

"What happened with Pete? I thought it was the hottest new romance to hit the island of Manhattan."

"It was. I just realized I was wrong about him."

"In what way?"

"He was only interested in sex."

Sam pretended to look horrified. "You're kidding! The beast." He started laughing.

Bess tried to laugh it off, but she was annoyed with him. He was being pretty insensitive. "It's not funny. There are more important things in life."

Sam walked over and put his arm around her shoulder. "I'm sorry. I was just teasing. Of course there are more important things. It's just that sex is right up there."

"Would you sleep with Kate?"

Sam tried to recover from his surprise by joking. She was familiar with his technique. "I'll certainly try," he said.

"But you hardly even know her! It's your first date!" She knew she must sound like an idiot to him. A real child.

"It's a helluva way to get to know someone," he said.

Bess wanted to ask him how many girls he had slept with. After all, he was a sophomore in college. There must have been lots of girls. Had he loved any of them? She thought about Margaret and was immediately afraid. She didn't want Sam to hurt her.

She got up to leave the room. They had the whole weekend to talk. She needed some time to think things over.

"I think I'll take a bath," she said. "Mom should be home soon."

He looked serious—a deep line forming between his

104

arched brows. "Did I upset you?" he said. "I was just playing, you know."

"No. I'm just beat. It's been a rough week."

Sam looked as if he wanted to say something but then changed his mind. Bess caught the sudden shift in his expression.

"Did you want to ask me something?" she said.

"No. Well, I guess so. It's kind of silly."

Bess paused in the doorway and waited.

"That guy, Pete. He didn't hurt you or anything, did he?"

Bess laughed. She was relieved to see that he still had some protective instinct toward her.

"Only my pride," she said. "Don't worry. I heal quickly."

He grinned foolishly. "I'm glad," he said. "By the way, I completely forgot to ask about Margaret. How is she?"

"Fine. She looks terrific. She asked about you."

"Will I get to see her?"

She searched his face for anything unusual. She felt silly. After all, they had known each other forever. Sam was just being friendly.

"She'll be over Friday," Bess said. "She wants to see you."

He smiled, and she immediately regretted her words.

"Terrific," he said. "I'm looking forward to it."

"Sounds great," she said. "I'll see you later."

"Later."

Bess closed the door behind her and had an image of Sam in a black cape, twirling his mustache while he drooled over Margaret.

"Jerk," she said aloud. "Sam doesn't even have a mustache."

She heard the key turn in the door and went to open it. Her mother's face was flushed and excited.

"Is Sammy home?" she said.

"In his room."

Ruth squeezed her. "Isn't it wonderful," she said. "The whole family together. Just the four of us?"

Bess smiled and muttered, "The five of us."

Her mother didn't hear her. She was already running down the hallway, shouting, "Sammy! Sammy!"

Bess stood in the foyer listening to their muted sounds of greeting and wishing the weekend away.

Chapter 14

Bess watched Sam's eyes widen in appreciation as she opened the door to let Margaret in.

"Hi," Margaret said. "It's good to see you." She turned toward Bess. "It's *always* good to see you."

Bess didn't blame Sam for looking at Margaret as he did. She was wearing a pale gray sweater that clung becomingly to her full bosom—no need for her to move to New Guinea. A skirt of deep rose fell to just above her ankles. The pointy tips of her black laced boots peeked from beneath the hem of her skirt. A dramatic necklace of brass and blue enamel showed off the bright tones of her eyes, while her dangling earrings picked up all the colors in her outfit. On anyone else, the combination of clothes and jewelry would have been too much, but on Margaret everything looked selected with exquisite taste and style.

"I love your necklace," Bess said. "Is it new?"

"Thanks," Margaret said. "I picked it up at a crafts fair." She fingered the weighty brass balls. "I love the way it feels."

Sam had stood by silently the whole time, gazing wonderingly at her. When he finally spoke, he had to clear his throat.

"Yes?" Margaret said.

Bess saw how she was savoring her effect on him—it was a *sight* to see.

"You really look terrific," he said. "I can't get over it. It's another girl."

Margaret smiled.

"We all have to grow up," she said. "My time was way overdue."

"But well worth waiting for," he said. "I just can't get over it."

Bess started to feel as if she were intruding. They were unable to take their eyes off each other. She could feel the vibrations between them. They just grinned at each other a lot. She didn't like the way Sam was letting his eyes rove over Margaret's body. Margaret didn't even seem to mind. In fact, she looked as if she were guiding his gaze to the most strategic locations. It was getting to be too much for Bess.

"Do you plan to stand in the hallway all day?" Bess said. "I think the living room might be more comfortable."

"Sounds great," Sam said.

"Great," Margaret said. "Are your folks home? I'd like to say hello."

"Dad's resting," Bess said. "He's been really tired lately. Mom's around somewhere. I'll find her."

Margaret followed Sam into the living room. Bess could hear them laughing as she walked toward her parents' bedroom. She practically collided with her mother.

"Mom?"

Her mother's face looked drawn and concerned.

"Shh," Ruth said. "Daddy's sleeping. Who was at the door?"

"Margaret. Is he all right?"

Her mother smiled and draped an arm across her shoulder. "Don't look so worried, honey. He's just tired. Where's Margaret?"

108

"In the living room with Sam. Why do *you* look so worried?"

Her mother directed her toward the living room.

"I guess I'm tired, too. Let's say hello to Margaret."

"You go ahead," Bess said. "I'll be in in a minute."

Her mother nodded and walked off. She seemed distracted. Bess knew she wasn't telling her everything. She couldn't put her finger on it, but something gnawed at her. She just didn't feel quite right. On an impulse, she decided to open the door to her parents' bedroom. Very carefully she turned the doorknob until it wouldn't turn anymore; then she slowly pushed open the door. Her father was sleeping on his back. His face looked gray but peaceful. His breathing was hoarse but steady. She felt suddenly afraid. There was no logical reason for her fear, but an icy coldness gripped the back of her neck and made the hair on her arms stand up. She stood for a few minutes in the doorway, listening to her father's breaths. Just as she was about to close the door and tiptoe out, he opened his eyes and turned his head toward her.

"Bessie?"

She darted to his side.

"Yes, Daddy? Are you all right? Do you want anything?"

He laughed softly.

"My goodness, sweetheart. What's come over you?"

She sat down on the edge of the bed and lightly brushed his cheek with her hand. He hadn't shaved that morning, and his beard was coarse. She remembered how he used to like to rub his rough cheek against her smooth one as she squealed in protest. Now she bent her face close to his and rubbed her face against his cheek. She felt as if she wanted to cry. Her father reached up a hand and stroked her hair.

"What is it, honey?" Carl said. "What's the matter?"

She rested her head on his chest. It had been a long time since she had done that.

"Nothing, Daddy. I'm just worried about you. You've

been looking so tired lately. You didn't seem right yesterday at dinner."

"Just a little indigestion," he said. "I've been working too hard. Why don't you let me get some rest? We'll talk later."

She saw it was a struggle for him to keep his eyes open and felt guilty for waking him.

"I'm sorry if I woke you. Are you sure I can't get you anything?"

His eyes were already closed.

"Positive," he said. "Just close the door behind you."

She kissed his forehead—it felt cool and dry.

"I'll see you later," she said. She stood and left the room. As soon as she had closed the door behind her, she could hear laughter from the living room. Her mother had joined Sam and Margaret, so she didn't feel too uncomfortable about going in.

Margaret and Ruth were sitting on the couch. Sam was stretched out in the green recliner.

"Bess!" Sam said. "You're just the one I want. Do you remember the time I took you and Margaret ice-skating at Rockefeller Center?"

Bess nodded.

"Margaret here claims that I fell at least a dozen times. I could swear it was the other way around. What do you think?"

She looked over toward Margaret, who was sitting on the edge of the couch, as if her answer were the most important thing in the world. Bess felt embarrassed for them—the same way she did when she saw a lousy comedian. She just shrugged and sat down on the floor.

"C'mon, Bess," Sam said. "We've been waiting for your opinion. It's a question of honor."

"Think hard," Margaret said. "I'm positive it was Sam who fell."

"No fair!" Sam said. "You're leading the witness!"

Ruth laughed and stood.

110

"How about some sandwiches?" she said. "I think there might be some turkey left over. How about it?"

"Great!" Sam said.

"I'm starved," Margaret said.

Bess got up. "I'll help you," she said. She turned to look at Sam. "I don't know if it was a dozen times, but you did fall a lot that day."

Margaret squealed. "I told you! I told you!" She pointed her finger at Sam.

"No fair," Sam said. "She's biased."

"She's your sister," Margaret said.

"Yeah," Sam said, "but she's your best friend."

Bess felt sick. She couldn't believe the way they were acting. It was like watching Barbie and Ken. It was too much. She followed her mother into the kitchen.

"Should I make some salad?" Ruth said.

"Whatever."

Ruth took the turkey carcass out from the refrigerator and placed it on the counter. She also took out a covered plate of already sliced turkey and examined it.

"Do you think this is enough, or should I slice more?"

Bess picked up a piece of white meat and chewed thoughtfully.

"I don't know. Whatever you think."

"Thanks a lot. Well, I'll just put this plate on the table. You can help yourselves. Slice some tomatoes and cucumbers. That and the stuffing and cranberry sauce should be enough."

"Are there any sweet potatoes left?"

"I don't think so."

Ruth hummed cheerfully as she worked. She loaded the table with plates of food and dishes.

"Margaret looks wonderful," she said. "I'm so happy for her."

Just as Bess was about to respond, Margaret walked in. Her hands were pushed down deep into the pockets of her skirt.

111

"Can I help?" she said.

Ruth smiled fondly. "No, thank you. Your ears must have been burning. I was just talking about you."

"Good or bad?" Margaret said.

"Always good."

Bess sliced tomatoes with savage intensity. Since when had Margaret become such an attraction? It was enough to make her puke.

"Can I help with that?" Margaret said. She stood next to Bess.

"No."

"It's so good to see Sam," Margaret said.

"He seems awfully glad to see you," Ruth said. "How are your parents these days? I haven't seen your mother in ages."

"They're fine. Mom's busy helping Dad at the shop."

"And Jane?"

Margaret laughed. "Still a pest."

"Well, everything sounds normal."

"Disgustingly so."

Bess had started on the cucumbers. Margaret picked up a piece and popped it into her mouth.

"These are good. Where do you get your vegetables?"

Bess rolled her eyes upward. Pretty soon they'd be exchanging recipes. She listened to her mother tell Margaret all about the "wonderful market off Columbus Avenue," that had "the freshest vegetables in New York." Margaret listened with rapt attention.

"I'll call Sam," Bess said. "Everything's ready."

"He's taking a shower," Margaret said. "He said he'd be in when he was done."

Bess resented the tone of ownership in her voice, but she didn't say anything. She picked up the tail end of her mother's sentence.

". . . so I told Carl, why don't we just have a small family gathering for once? It was really lovely."

"I know just what you mean," Margaret said. "There were forty people at my aunt's house. It was all done buffet, of course, but you could hardly hear yourself think."

Ruth nodded appreciatively. Bess took two slices of bread and spread them with mayonnaise. She piled the bread with thick slabs of turkey, slices of tomato, and pieces of lettuce. She slapped the top with the other slice of bread and nodded approvingly.

"Have you heard from Zak?" she said.

Both Ruth and Margaret looked at her in stunned surprise. She was already chewing on a big bite of sandwich.

"No," Margaret said. "I didn't expect to." Her cheeks had two bright red circles on them. "Is there any reason I should have?"

"Nope. Just wondering." She took another large bite.

Ruth looked at Bess pointedly but busied herself at the sink. Margaret looked at Bess, waiting for an explanation.

"Aren't you going to eat?" Bess said. "You'll feel better."

"Don't you feel well?" Ruth said.

Margaret sat at the table and leaned over toward Bess. "What's with you?" she said. "Why are you so angry?"

"Angry?" Bess pretended innocence.

Tactfully Ruth began to walk out. "I think I'll see what's keeping Sammy."

As soon as she was out of earshot, Margaret slammed her fist down on the table.

"What's gotten into you? Didn't you invite me over?"

"Lower your voice. I most certainly did, but I didn't think you'd fall all over Sam."

"Cut it out. You're just jealous."

Bess considered this a moment. "Maybe," she said. "I still think you're making a fool of yourself."

"Maybe, but I'm having a wonderful time."

Bess was immediately sorry. She was acting like a baby. Still, it was a funny feeling to see Margaret and Sam knocking themselves out to please each other.

"I'm sorry," she said. "I'll try to behave."

"Thanks," Margaret said. She looked relieved.

Sam walked in, trailed by Ruth.

"Couldn't wait," he said. "Is there anything left?"

"Plenty," Bess said. "Help yourself."

They took their time over lunch, reminiscing about old times. By the time the turkey carcass was picked clean, they were all very full and exhausted from laughing.

"It's been a long time," Sam said. "Fourteen years?"

"Well, let's see," Margaret said. "I was five when I met Bess, and I'm seventeen now. That's twelve years."

"Close enough," Bess said.

"Well, I enjoyed myself," Ruth said. "I could use a nap."

"Go ahead, Mom. We'll clean up," Bess said. "I can't believe Dad's still sleeping."

"He's very tired."

"How about a movie?" Sam said.

"Sounds good," Margaret said.

Sam went to get the paper and returned waving it over his head.

"Hey, how about the new *Star Trek* picture? Think we'll get in?"

"Let's give it a try. What time?" Margaret said.

"Five-thirty," he said. He checked his watch. "We have thirty minutes. It's playing right here. What do you think, Bessie?"

"Why don't you two go ahead. I'll clean up."

"C'mon, Cinderella," he said. "Give me a break. Go get ready."

"C'mon," Margaret said. *"Please."*

Bess knew they were both being sincere.

"Okay. Let's just clean up. I'm ready. I just need to change my pants."

Ruth got up.

"Have a good time," she said. "I'm going to take that nap."

"Thanks for lunch," Margaret said.

"See you later," Sam said. He kissed her cheek.

"I'll take care of everything," Bess said. "Go get some rest."

"Miss Efficiency," Sam said.

Bess gave him a shove. Ruth left the kitchen. They loaded the dishwasher and returned the leftovers to the refrigerator.

"Not much left," Bess said. She wiped her hands on a dish towel. "I'll go change."

Ten minutes later they were out the door and headed toward Broadway. Sam walked in the middle. Bess noticed how his arm brushed against Margaret's. She listened intently to his every word. As they turned the corner, it was hard to miss the line that wrapped its way clear around the block.

"Is that for the movie?" Sam said.

"Wow," Margaret said.

"And it isn't even a Triple X," Bess said.

They all laughed.

"Whadda ya think?" Sam said.

"Let's head back home," Bess said.

"I'm game," Margaret said.

"Maybe we'll try again over the weekend," Sam said.

Bess noticed he had directed his comment at Margaret. She tried not to feel jealous.

They walked back toward home more slowly. There was no need to rush. Sam did most of the talking, explaining about his decision to switch his major from psychology to accounting. Bess couldn't help notice how absorbed they were in each other. There was no reason for either of them to notice the ambulance that stood in front of the building. Bess froze. There was no doubt in her mind who the ambulance was for. Her father's gray face flashed before her eyes. With a cry, she started running toward the house. Sam and Margaret looked after her, bewildered.

"Bess!" Sam said. "What's the matter?"

"Hold up!" Margaret said.

Bess ignored them and continued running, praying that it wasn't too late.

Chapter 15

Margaret couldn't bear to see the fear in Bess's eyes. It had settled there the moment she had seen the ambulance in front of her building. Margaret didn't think she would ever forget the look of horror on her face. Even now, just thinking about it, she tried to shake the image from her mind.

"Do you want some coffee?"

She smiled at Sam's thoughtfulness. After all, it was his father who was being examined by a team of doctors.

"No, thanks. How about you? Can I get you something?"

Sam sat down next to her on the green vinyl couch. She slipped her hand into his. His palm was cool and dry.

"Are you all right?" she said. "You seem so calm."

He smiled and squeezed her hand.

"I'm very tough," he said. He turned his gaze away from her. "I'm glad you're here. Very glad."

She noticed a tiny vein pulsing under his right eye and quieted the urge to kiss it. Instead she reached out her free hand and touched him lightly.

"He'll be all right, Sammy. I promise."

He nodded mutely.

The coronary care unit at Mount Sinai Hospital was quiet. Following a preliminary checkup in the emergency ward, Carl Ellis had been transferred to this floor. "He's had a heart attack," Ruth had announced. Her face had been ashen. "We don't know anything else." With that she had disappeared, leaving Sam and Bess shocked into stillness. Margaret had quickly taken charge of the situation, urging Bess to sit down and giving Sam instructions to propel him back into action. It had been successful. She had hurried off to get a damp washcloth for Bess and to make several phone calls. Margaret had sat with her arm around Bess, gently rocking her. Now, two hours later, Ruth was conferring with a specialist while Bess had been sent home to get some of Carl's things.

"I should have gone with Bess," Sam said. "I never should have let her go alone."

"She needed to be alone," Margaret said. "Believe me. I know her. She'll be fine when she gets back."

"Did you see her face?" He shook his head in disbelief. "I never saw her like that."

"It was a shock. For all of us."

"No. It was different for her. She kept repeating, 'I should have known. I should have known.' What did she mean by that?"

"I don't know."

It was only a white lie, she reasoned. Bess had told her that Carl hadn't looked well at all early that afternoon. Now, she blamed herself for not having recognized that a heart attack had been imminent. Margaret didn't see any reason to share this information with Sam. It had been told to her in strictest confidence, and she wasn't about to betray that trust.

He searched her face and smiled.

"You're really very close," he said. "I never realized *how* close."

"We've been friends a long time."

"In a way, so have we."

She wasn't surprised when he bent his head to kiss her. She had been anticipating it since she had seen the appreciative way he had appraised her the minute she had walked in the door. It just seemed odd that he had chosen this moment, in a hospital waiting room, with his father down the corridor on a cardiac monitor, to finally do it. It wasn't that she minded; it just seemed strange. Still, she was happy to return his kiss. It was exactly what she thought it would be like—sweet but familiar, exciting yet comfortable. He was an experienced kisser. She sensed it in the unhurried way his lips grazed hers. When he finally pulled away, she felt foolish at the way her eyes remained half closed, and her heart hammered. She swallowed hard and opened her eyes.

"That was very nice," he said. He stroked her cheek with two fingers. "I'm sorry I picked such a lousy location."

She didn't tell him that had they been in a field of daisies with a picnic basket of cold champagne and caviar by their side, it wouldn't have been any better.

"It doesn't matter," she said. "It doesn't matter at all."

They were grinning at each other when Bess stepped off the elevator. She was carrying a small valise in one hand and a number of magazines in the other. She looked better than she had when she had left. Her color had returned, and she was smiling, but Margaret noticed the lingering fear that hid behind her gray eyes.

"Hi," Bess said. "Did Mom come out?"

"Not yet," Sam said. "We're still waiting."

Margaret also noticed the way Bess's eyebrow curved when Sam said "we." She also followed Bess's gaze down to his lap and realized that he was still holding her hand. When she allowed herself to look at Bess again, her lips were drawn tightly together, and she was no longer smiling. Stubbornly she didn't move her hand.

"We haven't moved from this spot," she said. "We would have seen her if she had come out."

"Are you sure?" Bess said.

"Positive," Margaret said. She was angry with herself for feeling guilty. It had only been a harmless kiss. Bess should know better than to think that they were too involved with each other to notice what was going on around them. "Why don't you sit down?"

"I'll go see where Mom could be."

Sam released Margaret's hand and stood. Unconsciously he wiped his palm on his pants and then put his arm around Bess.

"Why don't you sit down? You must be exhausted."

Bess's first response was to stiffen the moment she felt his touch; however, the concern in his voice and her own anxiety must have triggered something in her, for she slumped against his shoulder and began to sob. Sam embraced her and smoothed her hair. Gently he pulled her over to the couch and leaned her heaving body against his own.

"There, there," he said. "Everything will be all right."

Bess sobbed continuously. A large wet spot formed on Sam's shirt. Margaret searched through her bag until she found some tissues.

"Here," she said. She pressed them into Bess's hand. "Can I get you some water?"

Bess nodded. On her way to the water cooler, Margaret tried to imagine what must have been going through Bess's head when she saw Sam holding her hand. It must have been a very strange feeling—your best friend and your brother. How would she handle it? She wanted to think that she would understand, but it wasn't easy to know unless you were in the actual situation. What an awful day for it to happen. As if things weren't bad enough, Bess had to have this thrust in her face. Margaret wouldn't blame her if she never spoke to her again. She waited for the paper cup to fill and drank thirstily, filling it twice again. She crumpled the cup and threw it in the trash basket.

"Damn," she said. "Damn my lousy timing."

A nurse passed her without even bothering to lift her head.

"Damn," she repeated. "No one even wants to know why I'm so angry."

She filled a new cup with water and walked back toward the waiting room. Ruth was sitting on the couch. Sam still had one arm around Bess. He was listening intently to Ruth's words. Margaret hesitated—she didn't want to intrude. Sam looked up and smiled, and Ruth turned her head.

"Margaret, dear," Ruth said. "Come sit down."

"Are you sure?" Margaret said. "I can wait here. I really don't mind. I'd understand."

"Sit down," Ruth said. "You've been here all evening with us. You have a right to know what's going on. Did you phone your parents?"

"Yes." She was glad she didn't mention that her parents wouldn't be back from New Jersey until morning. They had allowed her to return alone because of rehearsals.

"Good. Now, come on. I have good news for you."

Margaret was careful not to sit next to Sam. Bess didn't even look at her as she took a seat beside Ruth.

"What did the doctors say?" Margaret said.

"Well, it's a warning. He had a heart attack, but it was very mild. In a way, we should consider ourselves very lucky. Some people never get a second chance. He'll have to stay here for a few days. They want to take some tests. We'll know more then. He's resting comfortably."

Margaret reached over and took Ruth's hand.

"I'm so glad. I was so worried." She struggled to keep the tears back.

"I know, dear." Ruth said. She patted Margaret's hand. "I'm so glad you were with us. We all are."

Margaret avoided looking at Bess.

"So, now what?" Sam said. "Can we see him?"

"I'm afraid not," Ruth said. "He's sedated. I think the most important thing is that he gets some rest. He knows you're all here. I spoke to him, and he recognized me. Still, he's very groggy. Let's give him until tomorrow. I think we should all go home and get some sleep."

Bess stood and tucked her blouse into her pants.

"I'll be right back," she said. "I just want to wash my face."

"Fine," Ruth said. "I still have to see one of the doctors. Why don't you all go on ahead?"

"We'll wait for you," Sam said.

Bess still stood near them. "I agree," she said.

"I can take a cab home," Margaret said.

"I'll take you home," Sam said.

On hearing that, Bess turned and left the waiting room. Ruth seemed not to notice.

"Sam," she said, "why don't you take Margaret home and then come back for us." She reached into her purse for some bills. "Take a cab. It's late. I don't want you wandering around in the middle of the night."

"Are you sure it's all right?" Margaret said. "I can wait. My parents won't be home until tomorrow."

She regretted the words the minute they were out of her mouth. Ruth seemed not to have heard her, but Sam had definitely registered the information. His eyebrow had the same way of moving up as Bess's did. It signaled surprise and interest.

"Please," Ruth said, "run along. You need some rest. Your face is flushed. I hope you're not coming down with anything. Get some sleep. We'll see you tomorrow."

Margaret and Sam watched her as she walked down the corridor. Her back was straight, and her head was high.

"She's a very strong woman," Margaret said. "I admire her."

"Yeah," Sam said. "She's really something."

"I'm glad your dad will be all right. That was some scare."

"We're not out of the woods yet."

"What do you mean?"

"I don't know. I just have a feeling that Mom's sort of simplifying things. Dad's in an intensive care unit—that's not a great sign. Mom says it's standard procedure, but I have my doubts. We'll just have to wait and see." He ran a hand through his hair. "I've had it. Are you ready?"

"I just want to talk to Bess. I'll be right back."

Bess was blotting her face with a paper towel when Margaret walked into the washroom.

"Bess?"

She didn't answer. She continued drying her face without turning to face Margaret.

"We have to talk," Margaret said. "It can't wait."

Bess crumpled the paper towel into a ball and aimed for the trash—she missed.

"I guess it's not my day," Bess said. "Is it?"

Margaret walked toward her and tried to take her hand. Bess took a few steps back. She felt her former sympathy vanish.

"Really, Bess. *I'm* supposed to be the actress. Don't you think you're overreacting?"

"I don't know what you're talking about."

"Come off it. I saw you, Bess. I know you saw Sam holding my hand."

"Holding *your* hand? I thought *you* were holding *his* hand."

Margaret had an urge to smack her right in the head. She tried to stay calm. After all, it had been a hard day for all of them, especially for Bess.

"Look," Margaret said, "I know you had a bad evening. I know this thing with your father scared the life out of you, and I don't blame you at all. It would have scared the life out of me if it had been my father. As it is, I'm pretty upset."

"How nice that Sam was here to comfort you."

She decided to let the remark go.

"I'd do anything for you, Bessie. You know that. You're my best friend, and you'll always come first."

Bess didn't look as if she believed her.

"Sam is going to take me home. I'll call you in the morning. If there's anything you need, call me. Don't worry what time it is, just call me."

Bess didn't respond. She looked at Margaret, but she didn't say a word.

"Well," Margaret said. "I'm going to go. Sam is waiting. I love you, Bess. I really do."

She hesitated a moment and then turned to leave. Just as she was about to push the door to the washroom open, Bess called her name.

"Yes?" Margaret said.

"Don't get involved with Sam."

"What?" She couldn't believe her request.

"You said you loved me. Well, if you do, don't get involved with Sam."

Later Margaret would go over the scene a dozen times. She established that it was to her credit that she had hesitated only a second before answering.

"I do love you, Bessie. The thing is, I have to be fair to myself. I won't do it. I'm sorry."

After she had walked out, leaving Bess silent and stunned, she leaned heavily against the wall. Her heart was pounding, and she didn't feel like seeing anyone. She tried to calm down by taking a few deep breaths. Finally, her heart beating only slightly irregularly, she rejoined Sam in the waiting room.

"I'm ready," she said.

"Is Bess all right?"

"She's fine. Just tired."

In the elevator, he pulled her against him and hugged her tightly.

"I'm really glad you were with me. It helped a lot."

She hugged him back. His sweater felt scratchy against her cheek.

"I'm glad I was here," she said.

They had no trouble getting a cab. There were always a

few that drove past hospitals periodically. Airports, hospitals, bus terminals, train stations—they all represented the comings and goings of daily life. Margaret quietly pondered this thought as the cab drove crosstown through Central Park. It was wonderfully still this late at night. She felt sleepy and rested her head against Sam's shoulder. He was very quiet.

"Are you all right?" Margaret said.

He nodded.

It was only a matter of minutes until the cab pulled up in front of her building. She waited as he paid the driver.

"I'll take you up," Sam said.

Margaret greeted the doorman. "Ralph," she said.

"Evening, Miss Manning."

Margaret busied herself searching for her keys. She was embarrassed to be accompanied by a boy this late at night. Ralph must have known that her parents were away.

Neither Sam nor Margaret said a word to each other as the elevator took them to the sixth floor. He followed her to her apartment and waited as she fumbled with the key.

"Let me do that," he said.

He took the key from her hand without looking at her. He opened the door almost instantly.

"Thanks," she said.

"Well," he said.

"Well."

"Aren't you going to ask me in?"

She stood in the doorway, holding the door open with one hand.

"I really shouldn't," she said.

He bent over and kissed her—longer this time and pulling her against his body. They smiled at each other as she closed the door behind them.

Chapter 16

It was still dark outside when Bess opened her eyes. She peered at the glowing digits on her clock radio—it was only five-fifteen. She had trouble remembering what day it was. Was it Saturday or Sunday? She had a vague feeling that something was different, but she couldn't fit the pieces together. As she moved from disorientation to consciousness, she remembered it was Saturday. The events of the previous day flooded her, and an image of her father hooked up to slowly dripping bottles of fluids propelled her into full wakefulness. She sat up and felt around under her bed for her slippers. It was chilly in her room, and she shivered. When she finally found her slippers, she pulled them on and was comforted by their familiar softness. Quietly she took her robe from the hook at the back of her door and crept down the hallway into the kitchen.

She found the kitchen exactly as her parents must have left it before hurrying off in the ambulance. It was as if she had been given an opportunity to witness the scene from a ghostly vantage point. Standing there silently in the eerie darkness of the early morning, she felt certain that she could see her parents moving about the room only moments before her mother must have dialed the emergency number.

The table was strewn with dirty dishes—she could see the remnants of the turkey sandwich her mother must have brought in to her father after they had left for the movies. She must have brought him in a tray, urging him to eat, certain that some nourishing food would cure whatever it was that was ailing him. How soon after Ruth had set the tray down on the table had Carl cried out for help? Bess's gaze lingered over an untouched piece of pecan pie that was on the tray next to the cup of cold black coffee. How had her mother felt at hearing her father's voice? She shuddered, remembering how cool and dry his skin had felt to her that afternoon. Why hadn't she known? He had been complaining of tiredness and indigestion all day. She noticed a bottle of bicarbonate on the table. It stood next to a glass of water. All the fizz had gone out of the solution, but a layer of powder had settled on top of the water, and particles of bicarbonate clung to the spoon that rested alongside the glass. He must have thought he had a bad case of indigestion. She could hear him telling her mother, "Nothing to worry about, honey. Too much turkey. You know how much I love your stuffing. Well, I'm paying for it now. A little bicarbonate, and I'll be fine." She could see her mother's lips pursed in concentration, unsure whether or not she should call the doctor. All the evidence of the day's events lay spread out before, mocking her. She felt weak and defeated. In an attempt to keep a hold on reality, she began to collect the dirty dishes and scrape their contents into the trash. Taking great pains to be quiet, she ran the water and rinsed off the dishes before loading them into the dishwasher. Her mother had left her purse and her shoes in the kitchen last night. Bess couldn't remember a night when her mother had gone to bed without first leaving the kitchen spotless. Satisfied that she had done something to help, she folded the dish towel and looked around the kitchen. There was no longer a trace of the events that had preceded her parents' hasty departure last evening. Feeling suddenly ravenous, she cut a huge slice of pecan pie and poured herself a glass of milk. She decided to take it into the living room and watch the sun rise.

The sky was just beginning to lighten as she turned her father's favorite chair to face the window. She sat down and put her feet on the windowsill. Realizing that she had forgotten to get a fork, she picked up the piece of pie and took a bite. It was wonderfully sweet. Her mother made the best pie in New York. Methodically, she took a bite of pie and a gulp of milk until both the plate and the glass were empty. She placed them on the floor next to her and pulled the chair closer to the window. On her knees, she could look down onto the street below. She saw a lone jogger run by. A man was walking an English sheepdog. She wondered how he managed with a dog that size in a city apartment. Several cabs drove by, and a police car cruised lazily up the block. She saw a few lights begin to appear in the windows along the avenue. It was officially the start of a new day.

"Couldn't you sleep?"

She turned around to face Sam. He was in his underwear and barefoot. His eyes were still heavy with sleep. She felt strangely peaceful and was annoyed that he had disturbed her mood.

"Couldn't you?"

He yawned loudly, stretching his hands above his head.

"Nope. I'm hungry. Any pie left?"

"In the fridge."

She listened to him as he opened and closed the utensil drawer. She knew which drawer it was because it always got stuck halfway out. She heard him lift it by the knob and rattle it a bit until the drawer was back on the track. She got up and returned the chair to its correct position and sat down on the couch. She drew her knees up to her chin and pulled her robe down over her feet.

"Mom really makes a great pie," Sam said. He was already chewing on a big bite as he entered the room holding a plate and the container of milk. He took a swig of milk straight from the container. "I can't believe how hungry I am."

"Don't talk with your mouth full. It's disgusting."

He swallowed and wiped his mouth with the back of his hand.

"Excuse *me*, Princess Bess. I seem to have forgotten my manners."

She looked away from him. She had a feeling he was going to say something about the fact that it had taken him almost two hours to get back to the hospital last night. She didn't really feel like hearing his explanation.

"Aren't you cold?" she said, hoping to distract him. "My feet are freezing."

He was careful to swallow his mouthful before answering.

"Just hungry."

"Mom must be exhausted. She looked beat last night. I hope she'll sleep late."

"I doubt it." He had taken a seat on a chair across from Bess. "About last night—"

"Maybe I'll fix her breakfast in bed. French toast, maybe. That's always been her favorite. Some strong coffee and fresh orange juice. That sounds like a great idea."

"Bess, I have to talk to you about last night."

"What time are visiting hours? I want to get there early."

"Bess!" His voice had risen several decibels.

"For God's sake, Sam. You'll wake Mom. Why do you have to be so damned selfish all the time!"

She had risen from the couch and was glaring at him. Her own voice was set in a controlled whisper.

"I get a sense that you're angry at me," he said. "Or is it just my imagination?"

She sat down again and folded her arms across her chest.

"I don't know what you're talking about," she said.

"Really?"

She knew there was no way out.

"Okay," she said. "Talk."

"I wish you'd be a little more receptive. You make me feel as if I'm six years old and I just broke a window or something."

"This is the best I can do."

He sighed and took a final swig from the milk carton.

"I really like Margaret," he said.

Bess stared at him without commenting. She knew it was awful of her to enjoy seeing him squirm, but she couldn't help it. She was feeling very vicious.

"She's a very special girl," he said. "I never really knew her before."

She continued to stare.

"Are you just going to glare at me?" he said. "Can't you say *something*?"

After a pause, she finally decided to speak.

"What would you like me to say? I know you like Margaret. I also know she's a very special girl. Is that what you wanted to tell me?"

"Why are you making this so uncomfortable for me?"

"Did you ever think that maybe it was uncomfortable for *me*?"

They scowled at each other. Bess would have been happy to put an end to the conversation, but she knew Sam was just warming up.

"I really like her," he said. "I mean, really."

"What does 'really' mean? You're talking just like a six-year-old."

"I want to date her. She likes me."

She got up and walked to the window. The streets were still pretty quiet.

"And you want my blessing?" she said. "Is that right?"

"I'm going to date her no matter what," he said. "I just wanted you to hear about it from me. Meg wanted to tell you first, but I said it was my place."

She flinched at his calling Margaret "Meg." They sounded awfully chummy for two people who hardly knew each other. Her best friend and her brother. It was so weird. Sam was still talking.

". . . we really talked a lot. She's very bright. I can't figure out how come I never saw it before. She was always little fat Margaret to me. Now she's a spectacular-looking woman. I can't get over the change in her. It's really something."

"What about Kate?"

"Huh?"

"Kate. You *must* remember her? The fabulous-looking chick you have a heavy date with this evening? The girl you've been dying to get into bed. Or did you manage to get 'Meg' into bed already?"

Sam colored, but she couldn't tell if it was from anger or embarrassment. She was furious with him, but more than that, she was scared. Had he taken Margaret to bed? Could she have yielded so quickly? Bess didn't want to think about it.

"What kind of guy do you think I am?" Sam said. "I told Meg about Kate. This thing between Meg and me happened so quickly, but we both know it's right. We had a good time together. It was so easy to talk to her. And whether or not we went to bed is really none of your business. Right now, we've got Dad to worry about."

She couldn't help feeling a little foolish. Still, he could be a little more sensitive. After all, it *was* her best friend. God, how was she going to face Margaret now?

"I'm going to take a shower," Sam said. "I think I heard Mom. Are you all right?"

She shook her head as if she were just waking from sleep. There were too many things happening at once.

"I'm fine," she said. "I'll try to deal with this. It's very new to me."

"It's very new to me, too," he said. "I think it's the first time I've ever been in love."

Bess was too startled to answer. She felt very lonely and very afraid.

Outside, the sun was shining brightly. Ruth had awakened shortly before eight and had two cups of coffee Bess had prepared. She had refused her offer of French toast, eating some dry toast instead. "My stomach is shot," Ruth had said, smiling wanly. By ten o'clock they were all dressed and ready to leave for the hospital. Sam hailed a cab, and they rode there, wordlessly lost in their own thoughts.

Dr. Fine, a tall man with tired brown eyes, was waiting for them when they arrived. He smiled warmly at them. He had been Carl's doctor for many years. Bess was certain that her father had shared his family's triumphs with him over the last years. Carl was very proud of his children. She felt a pang of fear. Dr. Fine ushered them into a waiting room. In a quiet voice, he explained that Carl had spent a peaceful night. He was still in Intensive Care, but that was standard procedure. There had been some damage to his heart, but he would recover and lead a normal life. Right now he needed plenty of rest.

"How long will he have to stay here, Doctor?" Ruth said.

"That's hard to say," Dr. Fine said. "One week, ten days. I can't be certain. He's very weak. He's also very scared."

He looked at Bess and Sam. He smiled.

"I know you're all scared, too." He patted Bess's hand. "I want you to stay calm. That's the best thing you can do for him. Why don't you go in to see him? He's been asking for you."

They all stood when the doctor stood. Bess thought it was amusing, but she didn't laugh.

"I have some people to see. I'll be in touch."

Silently they watched him leave. None of them sat down.

"Well," Ruth said.

Bess and Sam turned to look at her expectantly as if she were about to make an important speech.

"Well," Ruth said.

Bess started laughing, and they joined her. It broke the awful tension they were all feeling.

"He'll be all right," Ruth said.

"Yes, he will," Bess said.

"You bet," Sam said. He hugged them both.

They stood that way for a few minutes, hugging one another and laughing.

Bess had tried not to show how alarmed she was by her father's appearance. His face was unshaven. She leaned over the bed railing and kissed his rough cheek. He squeezed her hand and smiled. She had been happy when the nurse had asked her to leave. "He needs his rest," she had said in an authoritative voice.

Ruth had encouraged them to leave. "I'll stay here," she said. "I want you both to get some air. I need you strong and healthy." They had insisted on staying. Finally Sam had suggested that they take turns. He would spend the first shift with their mother while Bess took a break. She felt guilty about her relief in escaping. She felt stifled by the hospital's white efficiency. She spun through the revolving doors and into Margaret's arms.

"Oh, Margaret, it's you."

Margaret smiled, blushed, and lowered her eyes.

"How's your dad?" she said.

"Stable." Bess was eager to move on. One heavy conversation a day was enough for her.

"Where are you going?"

"For a walk. I thought maybe I'd head over to the museum for a while. Sam and I are taking turns."

"I know."

They both looked uncomfortable.

"Sam called me before," Margaret said. "He asked me to meet him here."

"I see."

"He told me he spoke to you today. I wanted to speak to you first, but he insisted.

"Sam's very stubborn."

Margaret laughed. "I'll say," she said. "He won't budge."

Bess bristled at her intimate tone. She knew it would take some getting used to.

"Sam's upstairs with my mom."

She tried not to notice Margaret's hurt expression.

"Will I see you later?" Margaret said.

"I guess."

"Would you like me to come with you?"

Bess considered the offer. She knew Margaret was being sincere. They really did have to talk about it, but it wasn't the right time.

"No, thanks. I'd really like to be alone."

She stopped to consider the truth of her words. She couldn't remember a time when the thought of being alone had been quite so inviting.

Chapter 17

When Bess shuffled into the kitchen shortly before noon on Sunday morning, she wasn't the least bit surprised to see Margaret at the stove.

"Good morning," Bess said. "What smells so good?"

"Blueberry muffins," Margaret said. "Did you sleep well?"

Bess tried not to show her displeasure with the banality of the question. Margaret looked like the picture of domesticity—she was wearing one of Ruth's aprons with the slogan FOR THIS I WENT TO COLLEGE? in bold red letters across the chest. Her sleeves were pushed up to her elbows, and her hair was held back from her face with two plastic clips. She was busy scrambling eggs. A pot of freshly brewed coffee was sitting on the stove.

"Are you all right?" Margaret said. Her back was to Bess.

"I'm fine."

"Are you sure?"

"Yes."

Margaret turned around and smiled. She looked annoyingly beautiful.

"Don't ask me again," Bess said.

Margaret heeded the warning and turned away from her.

"There's fresh coffee," Margaret said. "Can I get you some?"

She took her favorite red mug from the cupboard and poured herself some coffee. She couldn't think of a thing to say. It was strange to feel so uncomfortable with someone you'd known practically all your life. Yesterday she had been so sure about her feelings. She felt as if she had sorted everything out. What was wrong with Sam's dating Margaret? She had put everything in perspective and felt really good about herself. By the end of the day, she had returned home feeling as if a great burden had been lifted from her shoulders. Everything was going to be all right. She had congratulated herself on her ability to handle a difficult situation and fallen into an exhausted sleep. Now, with Margaret standing in *her* kitchen, wearing *her* mother's apron and cooking for *her* brother, she felt a kinship with the renowned ax murderer.

They were both grateful to hear a key turn in the front door.

"It's Sammy," Margaret said. "He went to the store."

Bess slowly sipped her coffee. She was uncomfortably aware that she was wearing a ratty bathrobe and her most unattractive pajamas. She pulled the belt of her robe tightly around her waist to hide the faded design of her pajama top. Normally she wouldn't have cared, but Margaret looked as if she had just stepped from the shower. Even in her faded jeans and old sweatshirt, she glowed. Wryly, Bess wondered if she had just stepped from the shower.

Sam was whistling as he entered the kitchen.

"My two favorite women," he said. He kissed Bess on the cheek and winked at Margaret. "How're the eggs coming?"

"Runny," Margaret said. "Just the way you like them. Personally, I find them disgusting."

"As long as you don't feel that way about me."

"Don't ever get runny."

"What if I get a cold?"

"I'll nurse you back to health."

They smiled at each other. Bess listened to their playful banter with a mixture of revulsion and envy. They seemed totally delighted with each other, yet she found their mating calls ridiculous. She knew that it was always like this in the early stages of a relationship. She had experienced it herself, but she couldn't believe that she had been as obnoxious as she now found them. She smelled something burning and jumped up.

"The muffins!" she said.

"Oh, no!" Margaret said. "How could I be so stupid?" She watched as Bess pulled them from the oven.

"They're just a little burned," Bess said. "We could scrape the top off."

"Don't worry about it," Sam said. "I bought some pastry."

Bess set the tin on the ledge of the sink.

"I can't believe the smell didn't wake Mom," she said. "I was sure she'd be out here by now, waving an extinguisher."

She saw Margaret and Sam exchange looks. Sam busied himself setting the cake on a plate, while Margaret served him eggs.

"Do you want some eggs?" Margaret said, turning to Bess.

"I hate them runny," Bess said. "Where's Mom?"

Sam didn't answer.

"I could make them hard," Margaret said. "It's no trouble."

"Where's Mom?" Bess said. She was beginning to lose her patience. She didn't like the way they had assumed a parental role. "What the hell is going on here?"

"Relax," Sam said. "Everything's all right. Really. Mom left early this morning."

"So what's the big deal?" Bess said. "Why do the two of you look as if it were some deep, dark secret?"

Margaret scraped the last of the eggs into a plate and put the frying pan into the sink. She ran cold water into the pan. Bess managed to catch a glimpse of her face before she turned her back—it was slightly flushed.

"Have a danish," Sam said. "I bought prune and cheese. Isn't prune your favorite?"

"Cheese," Bess said. "I'm going to get dressed. What time are you going to the hospital?"

She saw Sam look at Margaret.

"Well?" Bess said.

"I was going to go now," Sam said. "As soon as I finish breakfast."

"It's almost one o'clock," Bess said. "When did you get up?"

"Early."

"How come you didn't eat?"

Once again she saw Sam and Margaret exchange looks. She decided to ignore them. Instead she picked up a cheese danish and stuffed it into her mouth. She took her coffee and a section from the Sunday *Times* and bowed graciously.

"Well," she said between mouthfuls of cake. "I'm off to the shower. Are you going to wait for me?" She chewed slowly while waiting for Sam's response.

"I'll wait for you," Margaret said.

"Oh, I didn't know you were going."

"I was going to. Is that all right?"

"Fine."

"I'll meet you both there," Sam said. "I don't want Mom to be alone."

"Why didn't you go with her this morning?"

Sam slowly stirred his coffee.

"God," Bess said. "I didn't even hear the bell ring."

She tried to tell herself that it was her own paranoia that made her think that Sam and Margaret were behaving very strangely. Still, there was something about the way Margaret lowered her gaze every time she caught her eyes that made Bess very suspicious. Sammy hardly looked at her at all. Well, it was their problem.

"I'll be out in a few minutes," she said.

"I'll see you at the hospital," Sam said.

She finished her coffee and cake in her room as she pored over the travel section. She loved to read about the exciting vacation spots. Someday she was going to travel around the world. She thought of all the plans she had made with Margaret. After graduating from high school, they would have two months to travel. It was only a year off now. They were planning to backpack their way across Europe. They had even sent for brochures and youth hostel information. Now they'd probably never go unless Sam came with them. Well, forget it. *She* certainly wasn't going to spend two months watching them fall all over each other. She pushed the newspaper aside and stood up. She took clean underwear from her drawer and went to take a shower.

Under the hot water, she felt better. She let the stream of water beat against her back. She could feel all her muscles relaxing. She should have called the hospital before she got into the shower. Her mother would have called if anything was wrong. She couldn't seem to rid herself of the nagging worry that she no longer had control over anything. Her grandmother's voice stirred in her memory. "A horse has a big head; let him worry," Grandma Sarah always said. Bess laughed as she reached for the shampoo. Grandma had some of the funniest sayings. It had been a long time since she had even thought about her. Carl had been devastated by her death. It all seemed so long ago. How old had she been? Eight? Could Grandma really be dead nine years already? It didn't seem possible. She closed her eyes as she lathered her hair. "I never worry," Grandma Sarah would say. "I pay a man in Brooklyn to worry for me." She would throw back her head and laugh, pulling Bess close against her full bosom. She had been in her eighties when she had died, but her skin had still been smooth and soft. She had always smelled of Chanel No. 5. Even today, the smell of that perfume would cause her to turn her head sharply in its direction. She reached up to rinse her hair and pushed the suds out of her eyes. She really missed her grandmother.

As she stepped from the shower, she thought about her grandmother's funeral and shuddered. Her parents had argued about whether or not she should be allowed to attend. Ruth had been set against it, but Carl had intervened. "She loved Bessie," he had said, "and Bessie loved her. They have a right to say good-bye." He had been right. She hadn't been permitted to say good-bye to her grandmother because of hospital regulations. No one under fourteen was permitted to visit patients. "Even dying ones?" her father had angrily demanded of the nurse. In a way, Bess had been glad. She hadn't wanted to see her grandmother with tubes coming out of her nose and her arms. She had been sitting in the waiting room when her father had entered, red-eyed and pale. She remembered the way the vinyl couch had stuck to the back of her thighs when she had stood up. It was June, and she had been wearing shorts. "Grandma's gone," Carl had said. "She's gone." Sobbing, he had pulled Bess against his body. She had been frightened by the way he shook. She had not known how to comfort him but had hugged him fiercely.

Sighing, she now wrapped a towel around herself and twisted it into a knot just above her chest. It was too hot to dress in the steamy bathroom. She took her things and walked back to her room. Was her father thinking about his mother? In her room, she dried herself and pulled on some clothes. The funeral had been awful. It had been the hottest day on record for June. The sun was shining brightly, and everyone had sweated through the graveside prayers. She remembered the way her dress had itched around the collar. Her mother had pulled her hand away when she had started scratching with intense determination. She recalled the terror she had felt as she had watched her grandmother's coffin being lowered into the newly dug earth. Pressing her face against her mother's skirt, she had watched out of one eye. She could still hear the hollow thud of the coffin as it reached its destination. Oh, well, it didn't do to dwell on those thoughts now. Funny, though, that she should think of Grandma today. She had been especially fond of Margaret. "She's a nice girl," Grandma Sarah always said. She had loved to pinch Margaret's cheeks.

Those famous cheeks were not quite as fleshy these days. Bess found her sitting at the kitchen table drinking coffee and reading the paper.

"Did you swipe the travel section?" Margaret said.

"Guilty. It's hard to break old habits."

"Why should you have to break them?" Margaret set her cup down and leaned her head against her hand.

Bess took a seat across from her and picked up Margaret's cup.

"It's cold," Bess said. "I never could figure out how you could drink cold coffee."

"I like to sit with it. I learned it from my mother. There's more in the pot."

"No, thanks."

Bess felt uncomfortable every time there was a lapse in their conversation. She tapped her fingers against the table.

"I was thinking about my grandmother," she said. "Do you remember the way she always pinched your cheeks?"

Margaret laughed. "Do I? I can still feel it. She was something. Do you remember when she'd bake cookies with us?"

"You always tried to eat the batter, and she'd always tap your hands with that wooden spoon."

"Those were not taps! My knuckles used to smart for days. It was worth it. Those cookies were the best."

Bess studied Margaret's face. She couldn't figure out what had changed, but Margaret seemed different. She seemed so preoccupied. It was as if she wanted to tell her something but didn't know how to start. Bess knew she could help her, but she didn't want to. She didn't want to hear what she had to say. Whatever it was, she wasn't ready for any more surprises. Too many things had been happening lately.

"What made you think of your grandmother?" Margaret said.

Bess shrugged.

"I don't know. She had a lot of funny sayings. I guess my father being sick. You start to think about death, and—"

"Your father's going to be all right."

"This time."

"What do you mean?"

Bess stood and walked over to the stove.

"Damn," she said. "I left my cup in my room. All the mugs are in the dishwasher already."

"Use mine."

"Thanks." She took the extended cup, emptied its contents, and poured herself some fresh coffee. "Do you want some?"

Margaret shook her head.

"Let's face it, Meg. My dad's been sick for a long time. He's not old, but he's not young. I think about it a lot. Even before his heart attack. I always worry about my parents dying. Don't you?"

"I guess so. You've always worried more than I. Always."

Bess sat down again and sipped thoughtfully. "Why do you say that?"

"Because it's true. When we were little, you were *always* worried about things. Tests, sickness, school. I could think of a million examples."

"Did it bother you?"

"Obviously not. We've been together a long time, haven't we?"

"I'm afraid, Meg."

Bess's voice was very soft. She clutched the cup with both hands.

"I know," Margaret said. Her own voice was quivering. "I really do know."

"Everything is changing. I'm afraid my dad will die. I'm

142

afraid we won't be friends anymore. I'm afraid we won't go to Europe next summer. I'm just afraid."

Margaret shook her head. "You're too much," she said. "First of all, your father will be fine. He needs some rest and some time. He'll be fine. I swear it." She crossed her heart with her index finger and smiled. "As for us, we'll *always* be friends. Of course things are changing. They have to change. No matter what, we'll go to Europe next summer. I can't wait."

"Really?"

"Really."

They looked at each other. Margaret stood up and carried some dishes over to the sink. She grasped the edge of the sink and stood quietly. Bess had a sinking feeling in the pit of her stomach—she knew that something was coming. In a way she wanted to bring it about quickly and have it over with, but in another way she wanted to go running from the room with her hands over her ears.

"Are you all right?" Bess said.

Margaret swirled suddenly and faced Bess.

"I've been wanting to tell you something," Margaret said.

"Tell me something?" Bess said.

"For a day or so."

"A day or so?" Bess couldn't help herself. She felt like a robot that had been programmed to repeat only the key words. Her mind raced, trying to collect significant details about the last few days.

"It's about Sam."

"I sort of thought so."

Margaret turned away from her again. When she turned back, her mouth was set in a resolute line.

"We're still best friends," she said. "If Sam wasn't your brother, I'd have told you as soon as it happened. It just feels funny because he's your brother."

"Get on with it."

"Bess, I want you to understand."

"You have to tell me what it is first."

She knew already. It was just a matter of saying it now. They were in love, and they thought she wouldn't understand. They must really think she was blind.

"I slept with Sam," Margaret said.

Bess tried to pretend that she had misunderstood. It was just too absurd. They hardly knew each other. Well, they knew each other but not like that. It was just too ridiculous.

"Did you hear me?" Margaret said.

Bess started to laugh. She couldn't help herself. It seemed impossibly funny. Margaret and Sammy having sex. She just couldn't picture it. She became aware of Margaret's shocked silence and forced herself to stop.

"I'm sorry," Bess said. "I don't know what happened to me."

"Are you very upset?"

"Are *you*?"

They looked at each other. Bess realized that Margaret hadn't been prepared for a question like that.

"You don't have to talk about it," Bess said. "You really don't."

"But I want to. I just don't want you to feel funny because, you know . . ."

"Please." Bess held up her hand. "Don't go into my family tree again."

"Could we sit down?"

They avoided looking at each other. There was a new discomfort between them that made Bess ache with the strangeness of the feeling. She felt the inevitability of their separateness. They took seats across from each other.

"It's really bad timing," Margaret said. "I feel so lousy about it."

"About sleeping with Sam?"

Margaret blushed. "It even sounds weird. No, I don't feel lousy about that. I feel lousy that it happened with your father in the hospital."

144

"It would have happened whether or not he was in the hospital. That's hardly the point."

"Are you sure you want to talk about this?"

"It's up to you."

She felt strangely calm. It was almost as if there was relief now that the news had been broken. She felt more relaxed than she had felt in days. She leaned back in her seat and waited for Margaret to speak.

"I want to tell you everything."

"Spare me the details."

Margaret looked embarrassed.

"I'm sorry," Bess said. "I'm trying to deal with this. Tell me everything."

"Oh, Bess, it was so strange. I know it happened very quickly, but it seemed so right. I didn't plan it. I don't think either of us did. In fact, I think he was more scared than I was. I'm not sorry it happened. I'm just surprised. I don't know. Maybe it was too soon."

Bess controlled herself from asking a million questions. She wanted answers to all the questions she struggled with. She knew the best thing was to move slowly—Margaret would fill in the gaps at her own pace.

"Why?" Bess said.

Margaret shook her head.

"I feel confused about everything. I was afraid that if I didn't sleep with him, he'd think I was too young for him. It was stupid, because Sam isn't like that. He didn't push me or anything. It just seemed to be the right thing to do. He wouldn't have argued if I had said no. We talked about it. I wanted to do it. The thing is, I think I did it for the wrong reasons. I didn't trust myself."

"What do you mean?"

"I did something I wasn't really ready to do. I said I was ready, and I convinced Sam. He trusted me, so he trusted my judgment."

"I'm not sure I'm following you."

Margaret jumped up, startling Bess.

"You see," Margaret said. "It's not even the sex. That's not the big deal. It's the intimacy—the closeness, emotionally, of another person. It's very scary. I don't know if I'm ready for that."

"Does Sam want a commitment?"

"He wants something. It's not that he hasn't had casual sex—not a lot, but enough. It's just that he makes it very easy to want to be that close, but he also makes it very easy not to have to be. I'm only seventeen."

Bess understood. She understood why she hadn't slept with Lenny. She also understood why sleeping with Pete had been out of the question. Mostly she understood that it was all right to be unsure of her feelings. At least now she knew what she had been so unsure about.

"It'll be all right," Bess said. She reached out to touch Margaret's arm.

Margaret nodded.

"I'm starved," Bess said.

Margaret laughed.

"Well," she said, "at least some things never change."

They spent the next hour gorging themselves on ice cream, gossiping, giggling, and trying to pretend that their lives hadn't changed.

"Well," Bess said, patting her stomach, "I feel sick. It must be time to go to the hospital."

"I'm going to go home," Margaret said. "I'm bushed."

They left together and parted at the corner.

"I'll call you later," Bess said.

"Great," Margaret said.

At the hospital, she took the elevator to the Intensive Care Unit. Her father's bed was empty. Her heart sank.

"He's been moved," the nurse said. "He's on the fifth floor. Room 520."

"Thank you," Bess said.

She took the stairs to the fifth floor and arrived breathless. Her mother and Sam were in the room. Her father was sitting up, smiling and drinking ginger ale through a straw.

146

"There's my girl!" Carl said. "How's everything?"

She approached his bed cautiously. He looked very pale and much thinner. She kissed his forehead.

"It's good to see you up."

"It's good to be up. Don't look so worried. I'm going to be fine."

Bess sat on the edge of the bed and leaned her head against his chest.

"I'm fine, Daddy. I pay a man in Brooklyn to worry for me."

"I know that man," Carl said. "I know him very well."

Bess hugged him until he squealed in protest. As she turned her head, she caught Sam's eye. They smiled at each other. She realized it was going to be a long day. Right now she just wanted to stay nestled against her father's chest—it seemed the safest place to be in a world of endless uncertainties.

Chapter 18

Ruth had protested Sam's decision to stay a few extra days—she was worried about his missing classes.

They were sitting in the hospital lounge, waiting to see the doctor.

"School is much too important to miss," Ruth said.

"I'll make up for any of the work I miss," Sam said. "I only have two classes on Monday anyway."

"Are you sure? Are you absolutely sure?"

"Positive."

That had been the end of that. Bess knew her mother was under a lot of pressure—she *never* gave up that easily. Ruth seemed to have aged ten years overnight. The lines around her mouth and eyes were more obvious since Carl's heart attack. Even her hair seemed grayer.

"Are you all right, Mom?" Bess had asked when they were freshening up in the hospital ladies' room.

Ruth had laughed.

"Just beat, dear. I haven't worn makeup in days, and I missed my appointment at the beauty parlor. That's enough to cause anyone concern."

She had reached out and stroked Bess's cheek.

"You're still pretty," Bess had said. "I was just worried."

"I do look frightful. I'm going to make an appointment today. Lord knows, I might give your father a relapse!"

Bess was often startled by her mother's irreverence. She tried not to show it. Ever since she had heard her mother tell her father that Bess was "thirty-five, I swear, when she was four," she had worked hard to be less serious. It was an arduous task. In the last few days, Sam had encouraged her to "lighten up" at least a dozen times. Her mind spun with hundreds of thoughts: What would happen if Carl died? What if he had to stay in bed for the rest of his life? What if Margaret got pregnant? What if Sam married Margaret? What if her mother remarried *after* Carl died? What if . . . *What if*?

"What are you worrying about now?"

Bess looked up into Sam's smiling face.

"Where's Mom?" Bess said.

"She's saying good-bye to Dad. So?"

"So what?"

He sat down beside her and stretched his legs out onto the coffee table. It was covered with magazines and ashtrays. All the furniture was an awful green vinyl, and the coffee table was scratched. Even the curtains, faded and sagging, were awful.

"It's been a long day," Sam said. "You look as if you could use a nap."

"I could. I'd like to sleep for a million years. I can't even bear the thought of school tomorrow. I didn't do any of my work."

"I'm sure Mom'll write you a note."

She shrugged. She was restless. It would be nice to go home and relax.

"You know," she said, "if I were a hospital administrator, I'd spend some money on fixing up these lounges, or whatever you call them. They're so depressing. It wouldn't

149

even be a bad idea to put in a few cots. Maybe people would like to take a nap or something."

"Or something," Sam said. He grinned.

If anyone had asked what could have been the worst thing he could possibly have said at that moment, "or something" would have been the winner. Bess's face turned scarlet, and she practically jumped out of her seat.

"Is that all you ever think about?" she said. "If someone mentions cot, the first thing you think of is sex. Remind me to watch every word I say from now on. I never knew my brother was such a sex fiend."

Sam's knuckles were white from the intensity of clenching his fists. He had whipped his legs off the table and was hunching forward as if he were about to strike.

"Cut it out, Bessie."

His voice was low.

"Cut it out? You have the colossal nerve to tell *me* to cut it out? Boy, I can't believe you—"

"Stop it!" He had stood and was towering over her—a tribute to self-control, except for the rage in his voice.

Bess stood and faced him.

"How could you?" she said. "How could you—with my *best friend*?"

She heard the shrillness in her voice and wished she could modulate her tone. She always sounded like a squealing pig when she got angry. It could be very embarrassing.

"Lower your voice," he said. "This is a hospital."

"I don't care what it is. You just don't care, do you? As long as you get what you want, it doesn't matter who the girl is."

She knew it wasn't true. Sam wasn't like that. Even Margaret had said so. Still, she couldn't help feeling as she did. She wanted to understand, but she was so angry she couldn't control her feelings. She felt like a kid no one wanted on his team—the last one to be picked. She didn't like the feeling.

150

Sam reached out to take her arm, but she jumped as if he had touched her with a hot poker.

"Get your hands off me!" she said. Her voice had lost most of its fight, but he withdrew immediately. "Tell Mom I'm going home."

"Please, Bessie. Don't leave like this."

She looked at him and was moved by the pain in his face. After all, he was her brother. How many kids had he protected her from through all those years of playing hopscotch and jump rope? She remembered his teaching her to roller-skate. His face had the same concerned look it had worn the first time he had watched her glide down a hill. The sound of the ball bearings had hummed in her ears as the cars and buildings had become a blur of color. "Stay close to the ground!" Sam had shouted from the top of the hill. "Keep your eyes open!" How had he known that she had wanted to close her eyes to block out the terror she felt? She had been certain that she would crack her skull wide open—still, she had insisted on doing it. "I can do it myself!" she had insisted as he had tightened the straps across her feet. Sam, always gentle, had succumbed to her stubbornness, always eager to please.

She felt all the anger leave her. It was time to make peace—with Sam and with herself. The defiant little girl with the red cheeks was getting too big for such foolishness—she knew she would have to deal with that ghost privately.

"You're right," she said. "Let's talk."

Relief flooded Sam's face. He broke into a cautious smile.

"Whew!" he said. He made an exaggerated motion of wiping the sweat from his forehead. "That was close. *Really* close."

"Why do you insist on providing a commentary on everything that happens?"

"You're right," he said, bowing deeply. "A thousand pardons. Let's talk."

She smiled. "I'm listening."

She felt the same way she had the first time she had safely reached the bottom of the hill.

Bess had never been so happy to see a school day come. The weekend had been an eternity. The routine of the school schedule brought welcome relief. Besides, she missed being alone with Margaret.

"Sam's leaving Tuesday," Bess said.

They were walking to school. It was a brisk, sunny day. Their coats were open. Before long, the streets would be slushy with dirty snow.

"I know," Margaret said.

They were both silent. Their feelings were still too fresh for them not to feel awkward with the situation.

"Sam told me your dad would be coming home in a few days," Margaret said.

"That's right. He'll have to take it easy for a while."

The pauses seemed endless. Bess spotted an empty can in the street and began kicking it for the remainder of the block. The hollow sound of the tin against the pavement filled the silence between them.

"He told me—" Margaret said.

"We talked about—" Bess said.

They turned to each other and laughed. Margaret held up her pinkie.

"We have to make a wish," she said. "C'mon, give me your finger."

She crooked her finger and offered it to Bess.

"We haven't done this in ages," Bess said. She looped her own finger through Margaret's.

"Make a wish," Margaret said.

"I did," Bess said.

They were standing in the middle of the block, their fingers hooked together and their eyes squeezed tightly shut. Their faces wore a look of intense concentration. Bess was the first to open her eyes.

"What are you wishing for?" she said. "You only get one wish."

"I know. I just wanted to make myself clear."

They started walking again. This time there was no tension between them.

"Tell me about Sam," Margaret said.

"*I* should tell you about Sam?" Bess grinned and rubbed her shoulder against Margaret's.

"Be serious."

Bess linked her arm through Margaret's and squeezed.

"I never thought I'd hear those words from you, but I'll try," she said. She wrinkled her forehead and tried to recall the major details of her conversation with Sam. They had talked at the hospital for almost an hour and then, after a light supper, continued the conversation long into the night. Ruth had turned in early, leaving them to an uninterrupted evening of serious talk. They had both been exhausted when they had finally dragged themselves off to their rooms. Now Bess saw the concern in Margaret's face and wondered why it was there.

"He cares for you very much," Bess said. "He told me pretty much the same thing you told me—it just seemed to happen."

"Do you think he's sorry?"

Bess withdrew her arm from Margaret's and shifted her books to a more comfortable position. She thought carefully before answering.

"I don't think he's sorry," she said. "I think he's worried about you. He feels very responsible."

"He didn't exactly twist my arm."

"That's not the point, and you know it."

"I guess."

"Look, Meg. You said it yourself. You shared a very intimate experience. There're a lot of feelings involved. It's not even the sex—of course, I don't know any of this firsthand, but I think I understand. Sam feels, well, I think he feels as if he's hurt you in some way."

"I don't follow."

"I guess he thinks he took advantage of you."

Margaret groaned.

"God," she said. "That's positively medieval."

"I know," Bess said, "but I think I understand something I didn't understand before yesterday."

"Why do I feel as if I've approached the oracle?"

"And from a virgin, no less."

They laughed. In spite of their closeness, sex was never easy to discuss.

"Not forever," Margaret said.

"Well, for a while," Bess said.

"Smart move. Tell me what you think you learned."

Bess took a deep breath and started to explain.

"It's funny. I've been thinking it over since last night, but I haven't really put any of it together. This'll be sort of a trial run."

"I'm ready."

"I hope I am." Bess shook her head ruefully. "I guess for the first time in my life I realized that guys aren't really that different from girls. Do you know what I mean?"

"I don't think so."

"I hope what I'm going to say doesn't sound as strange as I think it will."

Margaret looked exasperated.

"C'mon, Bessie. Get on with it," she said. "You should really try out for drama. You've got a real knack for building suspense."

"By the way, what's happening with the play? I've been so busy, I haven't even bothered to ask."

"That wasn't a hint, you jerk. We can talk about the play later. Right now I'm getting set to wring your neck."

Bess stopped walking and turned to look at Margaret.

"Stand still for a minute," Bess said. She grabbed Margaret's arm. "I want to see your face when I tell you this."

Margaret stopped and looked very serious. She leaned

toward Bess as if she were about to reveal the secret of the universe. Margaret's head was cocked to one side.

"You look like Buddy when you do that," Bess said.

"Who's Buddy?"

"Don't you remember? That cute little terrier we used to have. The one that was run over. Remember?"

"Yes, I remember. In about two seconds, I'm going to collapse on the street. Maybe that way I'll get some attention."

"Sorry," Bess said. "You know how easily I get sidetracked."

Margaret nodded.

"I don't think Sam was ready."

Bess said it all without taking a single breath. She looked at Margaret for a response.

"That's it?" Margaret said. "That's the big revelation you wanted to share? Did I miss something?"

"Don't you see?" Bess said. Her voice was high with excitement. Her words came fast. "Sam may have slept with lots of girls." She saw Margaret's expression and hastily tried to explain. "I'm not saying he has, but let's just assume that he has—for argument's sake."

Passersby were looking at them strangely. They were in the middle of the street, staring directly into each other's faces with great seriousness.

"Let's walk," Bess said, "before someone calls the cops and has us locked up."

"Okay," Margaret said, "for argument's sake, we'll assume that Sam has slept his way across America."

"The point is that I think this may be the first time it's been more than sex. I'm not sure why. Maybe it's because he's known you all his life. Maybe it's because you're my friend. Maybe it's because—he loves you."

She said the last words slowly and softly, letting them sink in. Margaret didn't respond.

"I think," Bess said, "that Sammy's afraid of his feelings for you. I think it scares the life out of him. He could probably handle the sex—it's the feelings he can't deal with."

"Did he tell you that?" Margaret said. Her own voice was barely audible above the morning traffic.

"No," Bess said. "He didn't."

"What should I do?"

Margaret eyes were filled with tears when she turned to face Bess. She looked frightened and miserable.

"What do you want to do?"

Margaret stared down at the pavement.

"I want to take it back," she said. "I want to go back and do it all over."

They had approached the front of the school building. It was crowded with kids.

"You can't," Bess said. "That's the one thing you can't do."

"What can I do?"

"You can move on."

"To where?"

Bess smiled. "To wherever or whatever will make you the happiest."

"How's your dad?"

Bess was surprised to see Zak when she turned around. Her history book was jammed in her locker, and she had been tugging it for the last five minutes.

"He's better," she said. She continued, unsuccessfully, to attempt to free her book.

"Let me get that for you," Zak said.

"With pleasure."

In a matter of seconds, he had managed to extricate the offending book. He handed it over to Bess and shut the locker door.

"Thanks," she said. "I always hated history."

"Always at your service. I tried to call you, but the phone was either busy or no one was home."

"I know. How did you find out about it?"

He looked surprised. "From Margaret, of course. How else?"

It was Bess's turn to look surprised. Margaret hadn't mentioned speaking to Zak. For some reason, she thought that Margaret and Zak would be over now. She felt a twinge of allegiance toward Sam.

"I don't know," she said. "Margaret didn't mention anything."

"Why should she?"

Bess didn't have an answer to the question. She felt foolish.

"Are you going to the hospital now?" he said.

"I was going to go home first. I have a ton of homework. Why?"

"I thought we could talk."

"Where's Margaret?"

"Rehearsal. The play's in three weeks."

Bess slapped her head with her hand.

"I keep forgetting," she said. "Very dumb."

"No. Very preoccupied."

She didn't feel like talking about Margaret, and she was sure that was what Zak had in mind. She was pretty much talked out. Why was everyone so eager to talk to her? Since when had she become so sought after? Maybe she should think about a career as a talk show hostess.

"I really have a lot of work to do," she said. "I've got to catch up. Midterms are in a few weeks."

He didn't look convinced, but he wasn't the kind to push.

"I'll walk you to the bus," he said. "Is that all right?"

"Fine."

He held the door open for her as they left the building. She liked the way he moved—he seemed so comfortable with himself. He was wearing a dark green sweater that looked wonderful with his red hair and light green eyes.

"You look nice in that color," she said.

"Green is one of the few colors redheads can safely wear," he said. "I have that from a valuable source."

157

"Oh?"

"My mother—she's a redhead."

Bess smiled and tried to relax. She didn't want to get involved in this thing between Margaret and Zak. It really wasn't fair. Sam *was* her brother, and her first loyalty was to him. Besides, how was she to know what Margaret had told Zak? Damn Margaret and her secretiveness. It could be such a bore sometimes.

"May I interrupt?" Zak said.

They had left the school block. She had been so busy anticipating what he would say that she hadn't noticed they had reached the corner.

"You take the bus on Broadway. Right?" he said.

"Right."

They walked slowly up the avenue without talking.

"Look," Zak said. "I have something on my mind and three blocks to spit it out in, so I might as well get to it."

Bess didn't look at him. She picked up her pace.

"Hey," he said, "don't run. I'm not going to do anything. I swear."

She slowed down. "I'm sorry. Reflex response."

"I'm glad you're in such good working order." He matched his step to hers. "I told you I spoke to Margaret."

"Yes."

"Well, we had a really good conversation. I know she didn't tell me everything. She sounded really tired. It must have been some weekend, what with your father and all."

Bess tried not to let her face give anything away. Zak continued without even bothering to look at Bess.

"I got the feeling that something happened more than she was letting on. I know how she feels about your dad, but it was more than that. She told me she went out with Sam. You know, your brother."

"We've met."

Zak laughed. "I think it has something to do with him. I'm not asking you to tell me anything. I'd just like you to look after her. I know this is a bad time for you, but I don't think I can help Margaret with whatever's bothering her. I think she needs you."

They had approached the bus stop. She was completely thrown by what he had said. She stopped and leaned against a car.

"Are you following me?" he said.

She saw the bus approaching.

"Zak," she said, reaching up to kiss him on the cheek. "I'd follow you anywhere."

She turned to join the line of people waiting to get on the bus. Zak looked sheepish but pleased. She waved to him as the doors closed and watched him until he had become a tiny dot in the distance.

Chapter 19

It seemed as if the Christmas decorations had sprung up overnight. No sooner was Thanksgiving over than everyone was planning for Christmas. Every commercial on television was advertising a new "must" for the holidays—it was enough to make *anyone* cynical.

"I just can't see it," Bess said. She was sitting cross-legged on her bed, staring at Margaret.

"Quit looking at me like that," Margaret said. She was trying to apply mascara without smudging it. "It's just mascara. What can't you see?"

"I'm not talking about your makeup. If you want to look like a jerk, that's your business. I'm talking about the way people spend so much money for gifts. It just doesn't make sense."

"What do you mean a jerk?"

Bess threw back her head and laughed. "It's just an expression. Cripes, don't be so sensitive."

Margaret shrugged and returned to her eyes.

"You know," she said, "it wouldn't hurt you to use some stuff on your eyes."

Bess wrinkled her nose and shivered. "Please, give me a break."

"No. I mean it. You have beautiful features. Some shadow and mascara would really highlight your eyes."

Bess pretended to gag—she made horrible choking sounds.

"Would you grow up?" Margaret said. "You're impossible."

"Listen," Bess said, "when your beauty book comes out, I'll buy a copy. What do you think a good title would be? How about *Makeup with Meg*? I like it! What do you think?"

Margaret turned around and gave Bess a disapproving look.

"You're a child," Margaret said with a sigh. "A real child."

They both started giggling.

"Are we finished exchanging beauty secrets?" Bess said. "Can we talk about important stuff now?"

Margaret snapped her cosmetics case shut and turned around to face Bess.

"I'm all yours," Margaret said. "Speak to me."

Bess uncrossed her legs and stretched out across her bed. She put her hands behind her head and stared up at the ceiling. She remembered how when the lights from the street used to cast shadows across the ceiling it would frighten her. When had she stopped worrying about those things?

"Do you remember when I used to give you flying lessons?"

Margaret put her face in her hands and shook her head. "Please," she said, "don't remind me. It's too embarrassing."

"You used to give me a quarter. God, you were dumb."

"Me?" Margaret's voice went up at least two octaves. "Me? You were the one who thought you could fly."

"Maybe, but *you* were the one who paid for the lessons."

Bess closed her eyes and smiled. She could practically see herself and Margaret as they lay side by side across the bed, their eyes tightly shut, willing their bodies to defy gravity and move through the air.

"We were awfully young," she said.

"We sure were." Margaret's voice was touched with wistfulness. "How did your father finally break the news to you?"

"God. I don't really remember. I think when he found out I was charging you, he decided to do something about it."

They were quiet, lost in their memories. Bess thought of how she had been allowed to fall asleep watching television in her parents' bedroom. Her father would carry her down the hallway to her room. Frequently she would open her eyes and feel herself floating down the hallway. Finding herself in her own bed, she had been convinced she could fly.

"You know," she said, "I remember telling my father how I flew into my bed at night. I can still see his expression when I told him—he never laughed."

Margaret nodded.

"He never once tried to talk me out of it—" Bess said.

"Until he found out you'd started a business!"

"Well, you can't blame him for that."

"No. I guess not. How did he put a stop to it?"

"I remember one night he woke me as he carried me down the hallway. 'Bessie,' he said, 'I'm taking you to your room.' I put up a struggle, insisting I could fly. You know what he said?"

Margaret shook her head. She was listening with rapt attention. Bess turned on her side and rested her head in her hand. Her voice sounded soft and faraway—even to herself.

"He said, 'Someday, Bessie. Someday.'"

They looked at each other and smiled.

"Do you think this is the 'someday' he was talking about?" Bess said.

"Do you?"

"I don't know, but I think I'm getting close."

"Me, too."

Bess looked closely at Margaret. She had changed since the whole experience with Sam. The difference was practically imperceptible, but Bess felt it. It wasn't even a week since he had gone back to school, but it seemed as if years had passed. Margaret had hardly mentioned his name. In fact, they had barely discussed much of what had happened. She knew Margaret was dating Zak, but if he had mentioned his conversation with her that day she knew nothing about it. It wasn't that they weren't close anymore. In fact, in many ways, they were even closer. It was just that they didn't discuss everything in as much detail. They had become more private, more cautious, about their feelings. It made her feel funny—sad, but excited also. Some things were just too hard to explain.

"What should we do today?" Bess said.

"How about a movie?"

She made a face.

"How about a museum?" Margaret said.

"Sounds boring."

"Shopping?"

"Absolutely not. Why does everyone rush things?"

"I hope you're not looking for a profound answer, because I honestly don't have one."

"I honestly didn't expect one."

"Anyway, I didn't mean for presents. I meant for us. I could use some shoes. What were you in the mood for?"

Bess smiled wickedly and stretched her arms and legs out to their full length. She threw back her head and arched her back, imitating a sex queen.

"I'm in the mood to be ravished."

Margaret laughed and picked up a hairbrush from the dresser. She made a motion to throw it.

"Hey!" Bess said.

"Hey yourself. You'd be out the door in two seconds, screaming for your mommy!"

"Is that the voice of authority speaking?"

The playfulness left them. They were broaching serious

territory. They were obviously uncomfortable and a little embarrassed. Still, Bess felt as if the topic had to be pursued.

"Well?"

Margaret got up from the dressing table stool and sat down next to her on the bed.

"Would you believe that I thought of *my* mother that first time with Sam?"

Bess knew the question didn't require an answer. She waited for Margaret to continue.

"I tell you," she said. "It was pretty strange." She traced a pattern on the bedspread with her index finger, avoiding Bess's gaze. "He asked me to come up for the weekend."

"He did? When?"

"Before he left."

"No. I mean when does he want you to come up."

Margaret lifted her head and smiled at Bess. "After your dad comes home. He'll probably try to come in whenever he can for a while. I guess some time before Christmas vacation."

Bess tried not to act surprised. She sort of thought it would be Margaret doing the pursuing, yet she seemed very casual about the whole relationship—almost indifferent. Bess didn't know which side she should be rooting for.

"What did you tell him?" Bess said.

"I told him I'd think about it."

"Why?"

Margaret leaned her head back and slowly rotated her head. "I've got to start exercising more," she said. "My neck and shoulders are killing me."

"I guess you don't want to answer the question."

Margaret straightened up. "Just stalling," she said. "Why? I guess because if I go there I'd have to sleep with him. Anyway, I don't even know if my parents would let me go."

"Do you want to go?"

"Yes and no."

"Explain."

"I'd love to see him. I'm really fond of him. You know that, don't you, Bessie?"

Bess nodded.

"I just don't know if I want to get involved in a whole thing with him."

"Isn't it a little late for that?" Bess tried to keep her voice level. It was awfully hard to be objective.

"Only if I don't stop it before it starts."

"But it *did* start. You can't take back what happened."

"No, but I can shelve it for a while until I'm ready."

Bess didn't understand. She looked questioningly at Margaret.

"You know how sometimes you start reading a book," Margaret said, "because *everyone* says it's so good?"

Bess nodded and tilted her head to one side.

"Well, you read the book, but you just can't get into it. It doesn't matter why. You kind of put it away. Maybe for a year. Maybe for a few months. When you finally pick it up again, you can't put it down. I guess it's all a matter of timing."

"Sam isn't a book. He's a person."

Margaret reached out a hand and rested it on Bess's shoulder.

"So am I," she said.

"I'm sorry," Bess said. "I'm trying to understand."

Margaret squeezed her shoulder. "I know. Me, too."

They were quiet for a moment, not really sure of what to say.

"I guess this is what you call a crisis," Bess said.

"I'm glad it has a name."

Bess snapped her fingers and jumped up. "I just had a great idea," she said. "Let's take the ferry. It's not that cold out."

"Sounds great."

"I just want to stop at the hospital."

"Fine."

They went to get their coats and scarves, talking excitedly. It was a perfect day to take the Staten Island Ferry—cold and sunny. It probably wouldn't be too crowded either.

Carl was looking well when they reached the hospital. Ruth was sitting at his bedside, reading to him from the newspaper. She looked up and smiled.

"Hello," Ruth said. "You just missed Aunt Lynn and Uncle Fred."

"I'm still here," Carl said. "Aren't you lucky?"

"Very," Bess said. She leaned over and kissed him. "You look good."

"I'll settle for better," Carl said. "How are you?" He turned and smiled at Margaret. "I got your lovely card. Thank you."

"You're welcome," Margaret said. "I'm glad you're feeling better."

"I'll be coming home next week," Carl said.

They all smiled at one another. Ruth folded the newspaper and tapped it against her open palm.

"I'm really sorry you missed Lynn and Fred," she said. "We were reminiscing."

"This seems to be a good day for it," Bess said. "What about?"

"Do you remember that lovely story Grandma Sarah used to tell you about why you have the little indentation between your lip and your nose?"

"Wow," Bess said. "I haven't thought about that story in years."

"She used to tell it to me when I was a kid," Carl said.

"What story?" Margaret said.

"How did it go?" Bess said.

Carl pushed himself up and rested both hands behind his head. He grinned broadly and shook his head. "It's amazing how these things come back to you. Well, it went something like this. Before we are born we live in a beautiful place. I guess you could call it heaven. We spend our days playing with the angels. When we're called upon to leave, we protest. We're anxious about the journey to our new lives because it's something we've never experienced. Are you following me?"

Bess nodded. Margaret leaned forward in her seat and rested her chin in her hands. Ruth stroked Carl's raised arm and smiled happily.

"Go on, Daddy," Bess said.

Like any good storyteller, Carl paused for dramatic tension. He fluffed up his pillows and made himself comfortable.

"Could I have a drink of water?" he said.

Ruth poured him some water from the pitcher on his nightstand. He took a sip and continued.

"The thought of leaving everything that's familiar to us seems to be the most painful moment of our lives. Nevertheless, when we're called, we must go. The angels gather around, trying to ease the terror of that moment. We struggle. At the final moment, an angel presses her thumb down between our lip and our nose, leaving us with a permanent indentation and shoving us into our new life. We come into the world crying because we're afraid of leaving behind what we know for what we don't know. I guess it's a story of resistance." He paused for a moment to consider his own words. "You know, I never thought of it that way before. I guess we always resist change."

Bess and Margaret exchanged knowing looks.

"Makes sense to me," Bess said.

"Me, too," Margaret said.

Except for a couple who were busy necking, they were the only two people on deck. It was colder than they'd thought it would be.

"I bet they're not cold," Bess said.

"I'm sure they're not," Margaret said.

"It's everywhere you look."

"I guess so."

The skyline of New York gleamed brilliantly in the sunlight.

"It's really beautiful," Bess said.

Margaret made a sound of agreement.

"What did you think of that story?" Bess said.

"As I said, timing is everything."

"Right."

They rested against the railing and watched the water splash against the boat. The water was dark and murky.

"I'd sure hate to fall overboard," Bess said. "This water must be filthy."

Margaret was staring down into the water. She seemed not to have heard. Her forehead was wrinkled in concentration.

"Wouldn't you?" Bess said.

Margaret looked up. Her face was blank. "Wouldn't I what?"

"Hate to fall into this water?"

"I guess."

"What are you thinking about?"

"Nothing really. Well, I was thinking about how surprised your father was after he told that story."

"What do you mean?"

"It was as if he'd just understood the story himself. Doesn't that seem funny to you? I mean, he must have heard that story a million times . . ."

"So?"

"Don't you see? It means we're not crazy!"

Bess laughed and slipped her arm through Margaret's. "I didn't think we were," she said, "but I'm glad you're so relieved."

"I guess we'll always be changing," Margaret said. "Won't we?"

"Not only that," Bess said. "I guess we'll always be surprised."

Bess was exhausted by the time she got home. It was already dark out, and she had forgotten to leave a light on. She hated coming home to a dark house. Her mother was still at the hospital. She unbuttoned her jacket and threw it across the kitchen chair. She was starving. There wasn't much in the refrigerator—the last week had been much too hectic for routine things like shopping. They had mostly eaten out or ordered-in Chinese or pizza. She decided to fix something for herself and her mother. Nothing fancy. She checked the cupboard to see what she could throw together. When the phone rang, she was sure it was her mother.

"Hello?" She was about to ask if soup and tuna-fish sandwiches sounded all right when an unfamiliar voice reached her ear.

"Bess?"

"Who is this?" She leaned the receiver against her shoulder and searched the refrigerator for celery.

"David. We're in bio together. I sit behind you."

"Oh, sure. David. What's up?" She tried to picture him. He was pretty quiet. She thought he had brown hair. Was it straight or curly?

"I was wondering if you were busy next Saturday night." His voice sounded as if it had taken great courage for him to make this phone call.

Bess found the celery and closed the refrigerator. She grabbed the receiver just as it was about to slip from her hand. She tried frantically to think of an excuse.

"Saturday?" she said. "Next Saturday?"

"Saturday," he said. His voice sounded much surer this time. He was clearly certain "Saturday" was the right answer.

"Well, I don't know. Next Saturday, huh? Let me think a minute."

"Listen, why don't you let me know in school tomorrow? You don't have to tell me now."

Instantly Bess was able to picture him. He had curly brown hair and very nice eyes—brown. He had a nice smile. He always smiled at her when she turned around. She remembered him now.

"No," she said. "I'd like to go out with you."

"Next Saturday?"

"Next Saturday sounds fine."

"Then, it's a date," he said. "Right?"

"It's a date," she said. "I'll see you in bio tomorrow."

She hung up the phone and sank into a chair. Her hand flew up to her face and carefully touched the indentation between her lip and her nose. The space was very deep. She must have put up quite a struggle. Smiling, she stood up and started to prepare dinner. She couldn't wait to see Margaret to tell her about her date with David. Instead of waiting, she reached for the phone and dialed Margaret's number.

"Hey, Meg," Bess said. "Guess what? I just got shoved by an angel, and I didn't mind a bit."

About the Author

Phyllis Schieber was born and raised in New York City. She took her Master's of Literature at New York University and taught high school English for ten years both in New York and Connecticut. She also holds a graduate degree from Yeshiva University as a developmental specialist and has worked with children who experience multiple disabilities.

Ms. Schieber now devotes her time to writing and parenting. She lives in Westchester County, New York, with her husband, Howard Yager, and their son, Issac. This is Phyllis Schieber's first published work. She is currently working on her third novel.

FAWCETT ● JUNIPER

Y.A. Favorites from

NORMA KLEIN

Available at your bookstore or use this coupon.

____**ANGEL FACE**   70128 **2.50**
Sixteen-year-old Jason tries to cope with his parents' divorce, his siblings' idiosyncracies and his first romantic involvement in this funny, bittersweet novel.

____**BEGINNERS' LOVE**   70237 **2.50**
Joel is shy and unsure of himself. Leda is outspoken, impulsive and knows exactly what she wants. Together they learn the excitement and joy of new love and passion and the problems of being too young to deal with its complications.

____**BIZOU**   70109 **2.25**
A spunky French teenager learns some surprising things about her family and her mother's mysterious past during an adventurous trip to the United States.

____**THE QUEEN OF THE WHAT IFS**   70223 **2.50**
Summer was trouble enough for Robin with her father leaving home, her mother feeling inadequate, her sister seeing an "older" man. Now was just not the time to be experiencing first love.

____**THE CHEERLEADER**   70190 **2.50**

FAWCETT MAIL SALES
Dept. TAF, 201 E. 50th St., New York, N.Y. 10022

Please send me the FAWCETT BOOKS I have checked above. I am enclosing $.....................(add 50¢ per copy to cover postage and handling). Send check or money order—no cash or C.O.D.'s please. Prices and numbers are subject to change without notice. Valid in U.S. only. All orders are subject to availability of books.

Name_____

Address_____

City_____State_____Zip Code_____

Allow at least 4 weeks for delivery.   **TAF-20**
